Write It Right:

Exercises to Unlock the Writer in Everyone

* * *

Workbook #6

Units 11, 12: Brilliant Beginnings/ Extraordinary Endings

By
Susan Tuttle

Susan Tuttle

Write It Right:
Exercises to Unlock the Writer In Everyone
Unit 11: Brilliant Beginnings
Unit 11: Extraordinary Endings

Copyright 2011-2014 by Susan Tuttle
All Rights Reserved

Susan's website and blog: www.SusanTuttleWrites.com
Email Susan at: aim2write@yahoo.com
Follow Susan on Twitter: @stuttleauthor, Facebook and LinkedIn

Cover design by: Aaron Kondziela (www.aaronkondziela.com)

A WriterWithin Publication

ISBN-10: 1941465099
ISBN-13: 978-1-941465-09-7

Write It Right:

Exercises to Unlock the Writer in Everyone

Workbook #6:
Brilliant Beginnings,
Extraordinary Endings

Dedication

The first unit contained herein, **Brilliant Beginnings**, Unit Eleven, is dedicated to Bill Kemble, my biggest fan, who unfortunately passed from this life during the writing of this volume. Thanks for all the encouragement and the love and the hugs, Bill. And thanks for the best compliment I've ever received, that I "out-Elizabeth'd Elizabeth George." You're the best. Every phrase I write is for you. Though I know you're watching over me from "up there," I will always miss you.

Extraordinary Endings, the second unit in this second Workbook, and the twelfth in the **Write It Right** series, is dedicated to my first-year students: Brandy McKay and Golden Quill finalists Jan Alarcon, Liz Regan and Nancy Bodily. Your talent astounds me every week, and I'm so proud of you, new writers all, for entering the Golden Quill Competition this year. Your courage keeps me going, too.

Contents

Before You Begin

SUCCESSFUL STORYTELLING LIES IN being able to tell the story you need to tell in the way readers need to hear it. When we do that, we create stories that readers cannot put down. There are many steps along the way. The first three, Character, Setting and Story, are contained in Workbook #1. The next most important element, Point of View (POV), is presented in Workbook #2. Workbook #3 presents Plot and Dialogue. Scenes and Style/Voice are discussed in Workbook #4. Workbook #5 contains Conflict/Tension and Subplot. Here in Workbook #6 you will find the final two and, arguably, the most important of the 12 fiction writing skills: how to Begin and how to End your stories, so that readers smile and say, "I'm so glad I read that."

In the few pages that follow is all the front matter that most people simply skip. If you haven't yet used any of the other workbooks, please read what follows, especially the *Foreword* and *The Value of Timed Writing*. I know most people page by the front matter and dive right into the meat of the book, but these pages are important. They contain invaluable information you will need to get the most out of these lessons and exercises. But even if you have read it already, please at least skim through *The Value of Timed Writing,* to reacquaint yourself with the "rules" of each lesson.

And of course, don't skip the book list. These volumes are all treasures for your writing library.

Foreword

WRITING IS MY LIFE. I have a thousand stories knocking on the inside of my head, seeking the freedom of paper. I also love to learn, especially about writing and ways to improve my range and skills. But I'm not very disciplined when it comes to how-to books. If it's not a mystery or suspense novel, I lose interest quickly, even if the subject matter is fascinating.

I found that, for me, the best way to learn something is to teach it to someone else. So, four-plus years ago, I decided to start a group where I could teach what I wanted to learn about writing techniques. If nothing else, it would force me to read those "how to write" books I've been collecting.

I formed the *"What If? Writing Group"* through SLO NightWriters on the Central Coast of California. I began with a group of six writers of various writing skills and genres. We met once a week for two hours to explore in depth a specific aspect of fiction writing. I worried at first that, given the weekly commitment, the group would gradually peter out. But not only did they keep showing up, they started arranging appointments and planning trips around the lessons so they wouldn't miss any!

As the year began winding down, I was sure this group would go on its literary way, and I wondered how to attract a new group of students. But when the year was up only one person left the group, due to health problems. Everyone else wanted to repeat the course. We picked up three new members and started again from the beginning, not sure if the original six students would get anything much from the repetition. To the contrary, we discovered the exercises worked just as well as the first time around—and in some instances, even better. It seems that, no matter where you are in your writing journey, or how many times you do these exercises, they continue to work. Every time.

These students are now getting published on a regular basis, and winning awards in writing contests. In fact, three of us won first place awards in different categories at the Central Coast Writers Conference in September of 2011. One even came home with three prizes in the competition! For me, this was proof positive that the **Write It Right** exercises had a hand in unlocking the talent of every member of the group. That's why I added an afternoon class and 8 more students.

The writing successes of both of the *"What If?* Writing Group" made me wish I could reach more writers with the materials we'd used. But even if I taught classes all day, every day, I could reach only a limited number of writers—and all of them local. I wanted more than that. I wanted to reach all writers, everywhere.

To that end, I decided to collect all the lessons into a series of 12 little instruction workbooks, a full program called **Write It Right: Exercises to Unlock the Writer in Everyone**. This workbook is the last of the series. The first Workbooks (Character, Setting, Story; POV; Plot, Dialogue; Scenes, Style/Voice; Conflict/Tension, Subplot) are available in print from Amazon.com or directly from CreateSpace.com.

Introduction to Workbook #6

BEGINNING A STORY CAN can be one of the most frustrating parts of writing any story. These days, usually all we get is the time it takes readers to scan the first few paragraphs of our story. Those opening lines either get them hooked, or they move on. And the ending is equally important. There's nothing worse than readers feeling they wasted their time because the ending disappointed them. It leaves them cold. Or confused. Or angry. Or disgusted. Never the kind of reaction any writer wants, because that means they won't ever read anything of yours again.

I know, trust me. There are a couple of rather famous writers out there who I will not read again, simply because they ended the book I read quite badly. Took the easy route out. Wrote themselves into a corner and didn't know how to get out except by what felt to me like cheating. And I felt cheated, because I had trusted them with so much of my time and ended up disappointed because the story wussed out in the end.

But you can learn viable strategies that will help you hook readers at the very start and leave them with warm fuzzy feelings at the end, techniques that will make readers actively search for your next story. In this this Workbook you'll find eight ways to craft killer first lines and exercises on how to integrate those lines into dynamic first paragraphs and first pages. And when it's time to end your story, you'll have eight techniques to choose from so that your story makes readers smile with delight.

It won't happen overnight. It takes practice. But through these exercises you'll develop the skill to thrill your readers from brilliant beginning to extraordinary ending.

It doesn't matter what level you are: beginner, intermediate or advanced. These exercises cross those boundaries and address where you are now in your writing career—and get you to where you want to be.

These are not time-intensive sessions. You only need to **dedicate approximately 30-45 minutes** to most of the sixteen activities (though a few may take longer). Feel free to move at your own pace—one or two exercises a week or a month—but if you choose a fast-track pace, do give yourself enough time assimilate each lesson. It's best to have a couple of days between each exercise. (The *"What If?* Writing Group," which has used these lessons for over three years as of this writing, does one or two exercises per session, with a week between sessions.)

All you need is a timer and something to write with—pen and paper or computer and keyboard, whichever is most comfortable for you. For maximum results, you might want to pick up a copy of some of the books I've used to formulate these lessons, and which I will reference throughout the course. It's not necessary, though it does make understanding some of the concepts easier.

You can use this volume as a workbook, filling in the pages (though you will need extra paper to finish most of the exercises) as you work through the lessons. But it is best to use separate sheets of paper, or work digitally in a word processing program, so that when you return to the lessons as you feel the need you won't be distracted by previous answers to the lesson questions.

Always remember, this is an ongoing process. Writing is a dynamic art and life is a journey through which you are always growing and learning. Over time your writing will expand and deepen to reflect these life experiences. When you finish this volume (or any of the exercises in the other volumes), you can repeat each of the exercises again, just as we do in "The *What If?* Writing Group"(now renamed The *"Write It Right"* Writing Group)—which at this writing is just finishing its third year of repetition, with the same students. You'll find that the second, and even third, time around your writing will reach even deeper layers and take you to greater heights. It will be stronger, more compelling and more exciting.

It's a fantastic journey. Plunge into the exercises in ***Write It Right: Brilliant Beginnings, Extraordinary Endings*** and experience what it means to unlock the writing genius within you.

The Value of Timed Writing

MOST OF THE EXERCISES in this course are timed. You have a specified amount of time to complete each one, usually 15 or 20 minutes. Thirty at the most. That's it. Period.

Why timed writing? There are two major benefits to timed-limited sessions. As **Natalie Goldman** shows in **Writing Down The Bones**, timed writing exercises force you to keep writing. You have a specific goal and only a short time in which to accomplish it. You have to step out of your way, turn off your inner editor—who is constantly telling you you've used the wrong word, no one will believe that plot, your characters aren't "real" enough, etc.—and simply write. From your heart, from your subconscious instincts, from the place where your stories live. It's authentic writing that's scraped to the bone of emotion. It's compelling and readers will want more.

The second benefit is that you learn to trust yourself and your writing process. When we learn to put our conscious mind on hold and just let the words flow, amazing things happen. Stories emerge that we never knew were there. Connections get made that our conscious minds would never have considered. Best of all, our authentic voice emerges, announcing in clear, ringing tones, "This is who I am as a writer. This is what I need to say." Timed writing exercises will introduce you to yourself.

Timed exercises allow you to step away from your editor self and into your writer self because you don't have time to think. You have to just keep writing, no matter what comes out. It may be hard at first not to go back and correct that word, rethink that action, direct the flow, etc. It takes time to learn to trust your instincts. When you find yourself wanting to go back, don't. *Write* about wanting to go back until you return to the natural flow of the exercise. You can always cut out the extraneous parts later. That's what editing is for.

Timed Writing Format "Rules"

Read the lesson, make sure you understand what to do, then set your timer and write until it dings. Don't stop to think, don't edit as you go, just keep your pen moving or your fingers typing on the keyboard. If you can't think of anything at first, write about not being able to think of anything and just see what happens. Repeat for the next lesson. And the next, and the next...

Also, be aware that my use of the terms "character," "person," "people," "he" and "she" are meant to indicate the protagonists, antagonists and other characters in your stories, whether they be humans, animals or otherworldly creatures. Make whatever adjustments you need to make to each exercise, so that it fits your specific genre and character choice.

Note: An asterisk at the end of an exercise denotes that there is an example of that exercise from my own writing at the end of the section.

Recommended Book List

THESE BOOKS, AMONG OTHERS, have been instrumental in the formation of these lessons. Throughout the course I will reference the pertinent page or pages to read in the appropriate volume. Although you don't need these books to complete the lessons, the information they contain is invaluable. It will add to your knowledge and skills and enhance your learning throughout this series. And they will form a solid foundation for your writer's reference library.

I have listed the copyright year for each volume that I have, so that if you want to get the earlier volumes in this series, which often reference these books, you can read the suggested pages. How-to books are often updated with new examples and insights. If you obtain a volume published after the dates listed below, you will still get the same fantastic writing information. But because things will have shifted around in newer editions, you might have trouble finding the proper references for each lesson unless you use a volume with the same publication date as those listed on the next page.

Write Away by Elizabeth George (2004)

What If? Writing Exercise for Writers by Anne Bernays and Pamela Painter (1990)

On Writing by Stephen King (2000)

Characters & Viewpoint by Orson Scott Card (1988)

How to Write a Damn Good Novel by James N. Frey (1987)

The Novel Writer's Toolkit by Bob Mayer (2003)

Finding Your Writer's Voice: A Guide to Creative Fiction by Thaisa Frank and Dorothy Wall (1994)

The 38 Most Common Fiction Writing Mistakes by Jack M. Bickham (1992)

Make A Scene: Crafting a Powerful Story One Scene at a Time by Jordan E. Rosenfeld (2008)

And every writer's library should contain the following reference volumes:

*The biggest dictionary** you can afford (check used bookstores for bargains). There's no substitute for a good, print dictionary

Roget's Thesaurus

Sisson's Synonms (if you can find it)

The Elements of Style (Strunk and White)

Barron's Essentials of English

Unit 11: Brilliant Beginnings

"A... story is like a chess game: The opening is a huge part of whether you win or lose. The first sentence of a... story doesn't just "hook" readers, it also sets the tone and launches the plot."

~Charlie Jane Anders

THE MOST IMPORTANT PART of your story is the beginning—the first sentence, the first paragraph, the first page and, if it's a novella or novel, the first chapter. In actuality, most of the time all a prospective reader will look at is the first page. Some readers will only look at the first paragraph! If that little bit doesn't grab on and not let go, the reader will go on to someone else's story, another author's book. And that's a great opportunity lost, for both of you.

As writers, we often simply start our story where we think it should start, and keep on writing until we hit what we consider the ending. We don't often give those opening sentences, those first few pages, the attention they deserve. After all, we know our characters so well, it's hard to imagine a reader might not be immediately sucked into why Janie isn't bothering to go to school today, or why Bruce has decided to quit his job and move to Africa.

It's easy to forget, when something is so familiar to us, that it isn't equally familiar to everyone else. But readers don't know Janie. They haven't met Bruce yet. They don't know that Janie's teacher has been sexually harassing her, or that Bruce's brother has been missing in Nigeria for the last six years, and Bruce just received a clue to his whereabouts. If they knew the backstory, things would be different.

But as tempting as it is, we can't begin our tales with backstory. While usually interesting, backstory is often slow. And boring. For a modern audience, we need to **start with action**, with an inciting incident or at least an urgent problem that has to be solved **now**—*or else*. There's no room to get to know each other, to foster a relationship between the character and the reader, certainly not in the first page or pages, nor even in that first scene or chapter.

So, how does a writer make not going to school or moving to Africa so compelling that the reader has to know *why*? Has to know *what will happen*? And has to know *right now*?

First, by not setting the opening of any story in stone. Once we as writers detach ourselves from the opening we first visualized and penned, we can then assess if that is actually the best way for the story to start. Sometimes that opening scene works exactly as we first write it. Sometimes we can't write the true opening until after we have written the ending. Sometimes the best opening doesn't occur to us until we're somewhere in the middle. It is only when we allow ourselves the **freedom to re-craft the opening**, to change and switch and alter things and events, even to start the beginning at another place or time, or with other characters, that we can find the exact right opening scene for every story we tell.

Secondly, we need to fashion **a first sentence that takes a reader's breath away**. This sentence is called a "hook." A hook is exactly what it says, a device much like the fishhook that captures the nosy trout. For that is what our readers are, fish swimming in an ocean of books, nosing and nibbling at whatever catches their eye. If we can set a "hook"—a first sentence that grabs at the heartstrings, at a sense of wonder, or at the reader's curiosity—and then "bait" it with the juicy worm of a vivid and compelling opening scene, we stand a better-than-average chance of landing that reading fish.

It all starts with a brilliant first sentence. From there we go on to perfect the first paragraph, then the first page, and then the first chapter.

Crafting the opening of your stories is the hardest writing you will ever do. But it's also the most rewarding. In the following exercises, you will discover **8 distinct strategies** for crafting that indispensable opening "hook." You'll also find techniques that will help you go on to the first paragraph, and the second and the third, until the whole opening scene presents such an enticing lure that readers grab your story and read until the very end.

Unit 11, Brilliant Beginnings: Contents

Lesson #1: Discovering Your Preferences

HUMANS ARE CREATURES OF habit. Though we know that change is inevitable and that it fosters learning and growth, still we fight against change with all the strength we can muster. We want, no we *expect*, our days to be the same: We get up, shower, dress, go to work, come home, have dinner, watch TV, make love, go to sleep. It's hard to even comprehend a mix of days that are all different, a time when we don't know what to expect from one moment to the next. It's why retirement is so difficult for a lot of people; their routine has been interrupted, change and uncertainty become a daily fact, and until a new routine has been established there's anxiety and fear ruling their lives.

But the human penchant for routine can be helpful to us as writers. Understanding what draws us, what fascinates us, what comprises our routines, can allow us to work with our limitations and stretch ourselves into areas in which we normally would not venture. And when we need to start a new story at just the right place, being aware of our "ruts" and knowing how to get out of them will make our job that much easier.

Some of us are drawn to facts. Some to emotion. Others gravitate toward action, while philosophy piques the interest of still others. For some it's a sense of the unknown or mystery, a puzzle to be solved. Others find the juxtaposition of disparate images irresistible. Understanding the forces that influence the way you put down your opening words can help you adjust, twist, and rearrange them so they will do what you need them to do: pull in readers.

But how do we figure out what draws us as a reader, what opening lines so intrigue us that we continue reading on? We could spend days in the library, opening each book, reading the first line, then analyzing our reaction to it. That's often how we choose the books we bring home with us. A title first draws us, then the picture on the book cover reinforces that draw—or squashes it. If we don't put the book back, we will open it and read the first sentence or two, to judge whether or not the writing is "good"—however we define that term for our personal reading material.

But who has time to spend hours or days searching out opening lines in the library? We're writers, that's what we want to be doing. When we read, we want to read an entire book, for both pleasure and to analyze what works and what doesn't. We certainly don't want to read only the first line of a variety of books. Thankfully, there's a shortcut we can take advantage of, called the internet. We can quickly search out lists of opening lines to read, analyze and draw our conclusions from. The exercise that follows is a short form of that activity.

In the following 51 opening lines, you'll find the facts, emotion, philosophy, action, mystery and imagery that open some of the greatest stories written. The first 46 were chosen by the editors of *American Book Review* as they complied their list of the 100 best first lines of novels; the last 5 are my picks off my own bookshelves. As you read these first lines, consider which turn you off—and why. Which draw you in—and how? Which intrigue you enough to make you want to go out, purchase the book and continue reading? Which simply make you shrug and go on to the next one?

It's in the *why* that enlightenment lies. What is it about the lines that turns you on—or off? Is it the sense of mystery, the depth of the emotion, the dryness of the facts, the touch of philosophy? Perhaps it's the way the words are strung together, their lyrical quality, or the very terseness they portray. Or it could be the shock of the images painted, or the rush of action presented. What is it that draws you, that makes you want to continue on? Equally important, what does the opposite?

When we understand what pulls and repels us as readers—and why—we can then begin to incorporate that sense of urgency, of "hurry, turn the pages, read on!" into each of our story openings. And we can also tailor our openings to match the actions, events and personalities that populate our stories. Then readers won't be able to put them down.

Exercise #1: Discovering Your Preferences

(Purpose of Exercise: to learn where your natural inclinations lie)

READ THROUGH THE BEST First Lines listed below. Try to figure out when each of these were written (they run from 1850 to 2010), decide if they were written by a man or woman, and take a guess at the title and/or author if you can.

Then mark those which appeal to you the most. Is there a pattern? If so, what do you think it is? Do you gravitate more toward character, setting, voice, situation, intrigue, philosophy, etc.? If you could choose **only one book** to read based solely on these first lines, which would it be? Why?

Give yourself **25 minutes** to finish this exercise.

A gleaning from the 100 Best First Lines of Novels

(as chosen by the editors of *American Book Review*)

1. A screaming comes across the sky.
2. Many years later, as he faced the firing squad, Colonel Aureliano Buendia was to remember that distant afternoon when his father took him to discover ice.
3. Happy families are all alike; every unhappy family is unhappy in its own way.
4. It was a bright cold day in April, and the clocks were striking thirteen.
5. I am an invisible man.
6. The Miss Lonelyhearts of the New York Post-Dispatch (Are you in trouble?—Do-you-need-advice?—Write-to-Miss-Lonelyhearts-and-she-will-help-you) sat at his desk and stared at a piece of white cardboard.
7. Someone must have slandered Josef K., for one morning, without having done anything truly wrong, he was arrested.
8. The sun shone, having no alternative, on the nothing new.
9. Whether I shall turn out to be the hero of my own life, or whether that station will be held by anybody else, these pages must show.
10. It was a wrong number that started it, the telephone ringing three times in the dead of night, and the voice at the other end asking for someone he was not.

11. Through the fence, between the curling flower spaces, I could see them hitting.

12. 124 was spiteful.

13. Mother died today.

14. Every summer Lin Kong returned to Goose Village to divorce his wife, Shuyu.

15. In a sense, I am Jacob Horner.

16. Mrs. Dalloway said she would buy the flowers herself.

17. All this happened, more or less.

18. They shoot the white girl first.

19. For a long time, I went to bed early.

20. The moment one learns English, complications set in.

21. Dr. Weiss, at forty, knew that her life had been ruined by literature.

22. Ships at a distance have every man's wish on board.

23. There was a boy called Eustace Clarence Scrubb, and he almost deserved it.

24. It was the day my grandmother exploded.

25. We started dying before the snow, and like the snow, we continued to fall.

26. I was born twice: first, as a baby girl, on a remarkably smogless Detroit day in January of 1960; and then again, as a teenage boy, in an emergency room near Petoskey, Michigan, in August of 1974.

27. It was a pleasure to burn.

28. Miss Brooke had that kind of beauty which seems to be thrown into relief by poor dress.

29. I have never begun a novel with more misgiving.

30. Once upon a time, there was a woman who discovered she had turned into the wrong person.

31. In my younger and more vulnerable years my father gave me some advice that I've been turning over in my mind ever since.
32. It was a queer, sultry summer, the summer they electrocuted the Rosenbergs, and I didn't know what I was doing in New York.
33. When Dick Gibson was a little boy he was not Dick Gibson.
34. The past is a foreign country; they do things differently there.
35. Justice?—You get justice in the next world, in this world you have the law.
36. Vaughan died yesterday in his last car-crash.
37. I write this sitting in the kitchen sink.
38. Of all the things that drive men to sea, the most common disaster, I've come to learn, is women.
39. The towers of Zenith aspired above the morning mist; austere towers of steel and cement and limestone, sturdy as cliffs and delicate as silver rods.
40. He was born with a gift of laughter and a sense that the world was mad.
41. In the town, there were two mutes and they were always together.
42. Time is not a line but a dimension, like the dimensions of space.
43. He—for there could be no doubt of his sex, though the fashion of the time did something to disguise it—was in the act of slicing at the head of a Moor which swung from the rafters.
44. High, high above the North Pole, on the first day of 1969, two professors of English Literature approached each other at a combined velocity of 1200 miles per hour.
45. They say when trouble comes, close ranks, and so the white people did.
46. The cold passed reluctantly from the earth, and the retiring fogs revealed an army stretched out on the hills, resting.

47. They ate Jorgensen first.

48. Charlotte Bowen thought she was dead.

49. While swords of lightning slashed and stabbed murderously across the scarred shield of sky, Bart Minnock whistled his way home for the last time.

50. On the day his destiny returned to claim him, Ted Mundy was sporting a bowler hat and balancing on a soapbox in one of Mad King Ludwig's castles in Bavaria.

51. The doctor woke up afraid.

(#1-46, from the website: www.infoplease.com; answer key given in the *Examples From My Class Writing* section, page)

Lesson #2: Crafting the Perfect "Hook"

"HOOKS" ARE ACTUALLY EASY to write, if all you do is write that first sentence. When you don't have to connect it to an actual story or plot, it's easy and fun to jot down several really cool, fascinating opening sentences. It's the **connection** that makes for the difficulty in crafting the right "hook" for each story.

Why is that? Because when the sentence is connected to a plot or story idea, or to the characters and settings, we become limited in the way we think about the words. It's difficult to "forget" that this first sentence has to lead to and connect with the next sentence, and the next and the next and so on, until a cohesive whole is created. And that it has to connect to the plot, the characters and the action.

But when all we have is a simple sentence, our imagination is unfettered by any consideration other than to craft a sentence that grabs the reader. It can create a mystery to solve or tug on the heartstrings. Or it can instill a sense of wonder or incredulity. It can present a quirky, attractive attitude or shove the reader into the center of the action. All because it doesn't have to go anywhere else. It can stand on its own merits.

If & When, a wonderful (though, sadly, now defunct) literary journal, had a section it called "Orphan Lines"—those wonderful unique sentences that seem to pop up in our heads out of nowhere and connect to nothing in our repertoire. But we write them down because they are so fantastic, even if we don't know what we will do with them—if anything. They don't connect to what we are currently working on, or to anything we have planned for the future. But they are unforgettable, just the same.

Two of my "orphans," which came from my Opening Hook Backlog—the listing of possible opening lines that I keep adding to on a regular basis—appeared in the inaugural issue a couple of years ago:

"Relationships with dead people are so one-sided."

"The world stopped when Goren laughed, so he didn't do it very often."

Some day, the second orphan line may find its way into the beginning of one of my stories. I've already begun a story using the "dead people" one—well, I have the first two pages—and am playing with ways the plot might develop.

Two other opening lines that came from the exercises I do with my classes have now been attached to actual stories I am working on, though neither of those stories had been even thought of a few years ago when I first did the exercise and came up with the sentences:

"My mother once told me that death isn't the only way to die." (from *Scenes From My Parents' Marriage*, a novel in progress, the first page of which won the Lillian Dean First Page Competition for novel at the Central Coast Writers Conference in 2011)

"The minute Meleia saw him at the top of the garden, she knew her mother had died." (from *Destany's Daughter*, volume 1 of *The Unification Quadrilogy*, the first page of which won the Lillian Dean First Page Competition for YA novel in 2010)

Both of these opening sentences set up questions in the reader's mind, compelling questions that must be answered—by continuing reading. Why would a mother say such a thing to her child, and what does she mean, that death isn't the only way to die? Who did Meleia see and why did it mean her mother had died? And what will happen because of it? The only way to find out is to turn pages. And keep turning them.

Remember, all these opening lines came from the following exercise. They were not attached to anything at the time of creation, although now they open three of the stories I'm working on.

From this you can see that crafting a great "hook" for an opening sentence isn't all that difficult **if you divorce it from any story line or plot**. It's only when story details get in the way that it becomes a true chore to try to craft that indispensable "hook." If you sit down once a week and write out 5 possible opening "hooks," by year's end you'll have 260 already-enticing lines to choose from when you begin to write your story. If you craft 10 opening "hooks" a week, you'll end up with 520 sentences by year's end. Chances are, one of these sentences will be the perfect start for pretty much any story you come up with.

Exercise #2: Crafting the Perfect "Hook"*

(Purpose of Exercise: To explore ways to create "hooks" unattached to stories, characters or plots)

FINISH THE FOLLOWING TWENTY sentences to craft an enticing "hook." Don't worry about whether you have a story or plot to connect to these sentences. The purpose here is to craft a really compelling first sentence, no matter what the rest of the story might be.

As you finish the sentences, try to introduce a twist, reveal something unique or unanticipated, show that something is about to change, or delineate a deviation from normal life. You might also choose to identify a character in an unforgettable way, jump into the middle of an action scene, load the sentence with deep emotion or present a quirky character or character trait. Don't spend a lot of time agonizing over which words to choose. Let your instincts guide you and don't second-guess your choices.

Feel free to change pronouns, tenses, names, etc., as you need while finishing these opening sentences. Set your timer for **20 MINUTES** and begin crafting your sentences now.

1. If only I hadn't…
2. It started yesterday when…
3. The minute he saw…
4. If it hadn't been for Paris…
5. Call me foolish, but…
6. We should have locked grandpa in the attic before…
7. If Joe had only hated…

8. Uncle Seth came to town the summer I turned twelve and…

9. Shouldn't it be easier to…

10. I couldn't imagine…

11. The sun came out twice before…

12. The townsfolk thought it was a miracle, but…

13. If I hadn't loved him…

14. Relationships with dead people…

15. It was my fault that…

16. "Ain't easy to kill," Garth once told me, "but…

17. I thought I'd wait a few hours...

18. They ate...

19. Summer arrived full of...

20. Rage roared in every cell of...

Lesson #3: Eight Ways to Craft a "Hook"

IT'S SO EASY TO get stopped by "opening-sentence-itis" as we try to find just the right words to open our stories. We know how important those first few words are, how critical to snaring our reading audience. And it's that very importance that tends to make our minds go blank. We write and rewrite, over and over, struggling to find just the right combination of words that will make readers say, "Wow. I have to read this the story."

Very often we don't ever find the right words. We simply "make do" with whatever comes to mind. Or we keep on writing and rewriting. And rewriting. Sometimes we can get so caught up in searching in the dark, as it were, for that elusive first sentence, that we never even get to the rest of the story.

The first sentence is vitally important, probably the most important part of the story. It either stops readers cold, making them put down the story, or it draws readers in and makes them want to read on. That's a lot of pressure on the writer. It means hours and hours of frustration and work, writing, rewriting, scrapping and rewriting yet again.

The search for the perfect words can even trigger writer's block. I sometimes wonder how many stories there are stuffed in writers' drawers or dumped in ignored computer folders, languishing from the lack of a good opening. I do know there are a lot of stories out there published with less-than-optimal openings. Because it's so hard to craft the perfect opening, many writers don't bother. They simply go with whatever comes to mind, with little thought about how those first few words will impact their prospective audience. Or they just give up after a dozen or so versions of the opening and hope that what they have will be good enough. Unfortunately, at best they end up with openings that are anemic. At worst, the openings will actually turn off readers.

But we want readers to read our stories. That is, after all, the biggest part of why we do this work; if we didn't want *someone* to read them, there'd be no point at all in writing down our stories. hey could simply say snug in our heads. We can have the most intriguing plot ever devised, the most enticing characters and fascinating settings, the most lyrical flow of words, but if no one reads past that first sentence, who will ever know? Who will ever care? It's more than worth the time and effort to craft a truly amazing opening for each and every story we write, no matter how long it takes.

So, how do you find the right opening for a story? Is it simply a matter of writing and rewriting the opening—over and over, sometimes for months—until by luck or elimination we just happen to hit on the right combination of words, images and tension? If we ever do, that is.

No. It isn't just luck that makes a great opening. Skillful writing is essential, yes, as is taking the time to fully craft the opening, but hours of writing and rewriting is not all there is to help us to find that amazing first sentence. If it were, very few books would have amazing openings. There is practical help out there, in the form of eight specific strategies we can use to find that magical combination of consonants and vowels, images and tension that will reach out, grab readers and not let them go.

The first four were identified by Camy Tang, who advises that we look for something unique and different in the opening situation in which your hero will find him- or herself. These are great strategies for action stories, mysteries, fantasies, any story where place and situation take the front seat. The second set of four were identified by Suzanne Pitner, and revolve more around the unique characteristics of the characters in your tales. These work wonderfully for character-driven tales, general and literary fiction and creative non-fiction. These strategies pique curiosity, shock or surprise, hint at future events, intrigue the mind or tug at heart strings.

Depending on the way your story unfolds, one of these eight strategies will no doubt fit in perfectly with your plot. Once you identify the strategy best suited for the story, you will have a framework on which to attach your words and writing skill—a huge step forward in finalizing the perfect opening for each and every story.

8 Strategies for Story Hooks — With Examples

1. **Introduce Something Unique:** "Rafe Noble, two-time world champion bull rider and current king of the gold buckle, never met a bull that he feared." *Taming Rafe* by Susan May Warren; "He always read the paper a day late." *Yesterday's Paper*, a flash fiction story by Susan Tuttle

2. **Reveal Something Unanticipated:** "To say that I met Nicholas Brisbane over my husband's dead body is not entirely accurate." *Silent in the Grave* by Deanna Raybourn; "I stood in the dark alley with a dead gun in my hand and smoking body at my feet." *Not Again,* a short-short story by Susan Tuttle

3. **Show A Deviation From the Norm:** "I couldn't imagine more shocking news." *A Proper Pursuit* by Lynn Austin; "They ate Jorgensen first." *Plague Year* (Volume I of the *Plague Series*) by Jeff Carlson.

4. **Indicate something About to Change:** "Any man going on this mission wasn't coming back." *Amber Moon* by Bradilyn Collins

5. **Identify a Unique Character:** "If Annabelle hadn't found a body lying under 'Sherman,' she wouldn't have been late for her appointment with the Python." *Match Me If You Can*, by Susan Elizabeth Phillips

6. **Jump into the Action:** "When the first bullet hit my chest, I thought of my daughter." No *Second Chance* by Harlan Coben; "She knew it was bad the minute she hit the water." *A Deadly Shade of Gray* (YA novel in process) by Susan Tuttle

7. **Pack it with Emotion:** "I cannot believe I'm standing in the exact spot where I was standing when I killed my mother." *No Place Like Home* by Mary Higgins Clark; "The minute Meleia saw him at the top of the garden, she knew her mother had died." *Destany's Daughter* (in process) by Susan Tuttle

8. **Show an Attitude or Quirk:** "By the time she was eight, Mackensie Elliot had been married fourteen times." *Vision in White*, by Nora Roberts. "I never thought I'd find love at the end of a gun barrel." *Dead Ringer*, a novella by Susan Tuttle

As you can see, each one of these opening lines sets up in the reader's mind **a series of questions that must be answered**: Will Rafe finally meet a bull that will make him afraid? What was the news that was so shocking? Who is Annabelle and what in heaven's name is going on with her? Killed your own mother? How? And why? Married fourteen times by the age of eight? How is that possible?

That is the aim of the opening sentence of any story, to set up questions in the reader's mind that **must** be answered. It is the **need to know** that drives readers to continue reading. When you **pack your opening sentence with a question that must be answered**, readers will have to keep reading to find the answer. And when you do it in a way that is memorable, breath-taking, thought-provoking, astonishing or poignant, it becomes unforgettable in itself even as it thrusts readers on into the story.

Utilizing one of the eight Opening Line Strategies as a framework for your story openings will give you the help and direction you need to find those all-important, elusive words that will grab your audience and make them need to continue reading to the very end.

*Exercise #3: Eight Ways to Craft a "Hook"**

(Purpose of Exercise: To explore the 8 "hook" crafting techniques)

WRITE A POSSIBLE OPENING sentence for each of the eight opening sentence strategies listed below that could be used to begin **eight different stories**. Analyze your stories in progress, stories you are considering, or make up story ideas for this exercise. Or any combination of these. Make the opening line for each story fit one of the strategies listed below, until you have used all eight of the strategies. When you have finished, you will have an opening sentence for eight different stories or story ideas.

Concentrate on infusing each opening sentence with the specific technique noted below, starting with those identified by Camy Tang, and going on to those identified by Suzanne Pitner.

Techniques from Camy Tang:
> A. Introduce something unique happening
> B. Reveal something unanticipated
> C. Show a deviation from the norm
> D. Indicate something is about to change

Techniques from Suzanne Pitner:
> E. Identify a character
> F. Start in the middle of the action
> G. Pack the first line with emotion
> H. Show the main character's attitude or quirk

Give yourself **15 MINUTES** to finish this exercise.

Lesson #4: Eight "Hooks" for One Story

WE CAN WORK VERY hard to find the one perfect opening sentence for our stories. We might rewrite that all-important opening dozens or even a hundred times, sometimes starting the story here and sometimes there, before we are satisfied we have it "right." But here's the kicker: Depending on how the plot unfolds, the characters' motivations, and the voice of the writer, there can be more than one "right" opening sentence for each story.

Yes, that's right. There isn't just one perfect opening sentence. Each story has any number of great openings just waiting to be discovered. It's true; more than one opening can contain an equally effective "hook" for the reader. And if we don't search for them all, we can't possibly choose **the very best one** for each story.

Too often writers will go with the first good opening they discover, without considering that there may be an even better way to pull readers into the story. Or a more effective way to foreshadow events, elicit emotion, portray action, etc. A lot depends on the story, on the way the plot unfolds, how the characters change and grow, and the theme or message contained in the pages.

It might seem obvious, when we start out, that a story that hinges on character development and emotion should have an emotional hook for the first sentence. That's logical and practical, right? And an emotional hook can very well be effective at pulling readers into the story. But one based on surprise could be equally effective, or perhaps even more so since it its very unexpectedness may pique readers' interest even higher. Or perhaps a jump into the middle of the action will push the opening up yet another notch. The juxtaposition of two disparate images, a twist of philosophy, or the foreshadowing of future events might make the opening that much more memorable than the emotional evocation we first thought of.

It's hard, when we feel we've finally found that perfect opening sentence—or even just one that will do well enough—to then experiment with other openings. After all, why argue with success, right? But playing with our opening sentences can have a huge payoff because, when we do keep searching, we often discover that one special combination of words that is truly unforgettable instead of merely adequate.

Consider the shocking **four-word opening** to Jeff Carlson's *Plague Year*, an astounding opening that has haunted many readers for a long time after the book was finished and closed: *They ate Jorgenson first*. It's not an opening that simply hooks readers and then vanishes into the bulk of the story. It's **four words** that keeps the shocking image of cannibalism in the forefront of the mind, and the need to know what is happening excruciatingly close to the surface, four words that haunt readers even after the reading is done. It's the kind of opening that echoes in one's head and surfaces at odd moments, and leads to readers saying to others, "Have you read *Plague Year*? Oh, you have to read it!"

And what writer doesn't want that kind of word-of-mouth? In this digital age of social media and the dearth of brick-and-mortar book outlets, word-of-mouth is worth its weight in gold. It's what sells books for us, perhaps more so than all of our other social media efforts combined. In fact, that is what social media is aimed at: increasing word-of-mouth. So it's well worth the time it takes to play with our words to discover that exact right combination that will not only hook readers, but also make them remember and talk about our work.

And it's not that hard to play with openings, after all. We have eight strategies to help focus our thoughts and direct our words, the same eight strategies we used in the last exercise. All we need do is **direct them all at one story**, instead of at eight different ones.

To do this requires us to look at our story from different perspectives, much like the blind men who describe an elephant after touching a part of its body. You remember that story: One patted a leg and said the elephant was like a pillar; one fingered an ear and said it was like a hand fan. Another stroked the tail and said it was like a rope, one felt the trunk and said it was like a tree branch, another the belly and said the elephant was like a wall. The last one touched the tusk and said it was like a solid pipe.

The thing is, *all of them were right*. It was their **perspective** that was different, that led to differing conclusions. The same principle—looking at a story opening with each of the eight Opening Strategies in mind—can be brought to bear on the opening of each of our stories in order to find the one perspective above all others that will be the **most memorable and unique** for our readers. When we shift our perspective and come at the opening from a variety of different directions, we can discover opportunities that might otherwise be invisible to us, just as the bulk of the elephant was invisible to the blind men. Then we can put together words that will have readers telling all their friends, "You have to read this story, it has the best opening."

*Exercise #4: Eight "Hooks" for One Story**

(Purpose of Exercise: To craft a variety of "hooks" for the same story)

Think of a story to use for this exercise. You can use one you are already working on, or one you have been thinking about starting, or create a new one for this exercise. Then, using each of the strategies listed below, write 8 possible first sentences for this same story.

Spend a few minutes considering the different events that might happen in the story, and who the character are. Then write eight different opening sentences, each using one of the strategies for crafting opening "hooks."

A. Introduce something unique happening

B. Reveal something unanticipated

C. Show a deviation from the norm

D. Indicate something is about to change

E. Identify a character

F. Start in the middle of the action

G. Pack the first line with emotion

H. Show the main character's attitude or quirk

Give yourself **15 minutes** to complete this exercise. Find your story idea and begin now.

Lesson #5: First Paragraphs From Given Beginnings

CRAFTING THE "HOOK" SENTENCE is only one part of creating a compelling opening to your story. After you get that amazing first sentence hook, each sentence of the first paragraph (and the whole first page and first chapter, for that matter) must draw the readers into at least **one aspect of the story**.

What makes a paragraph? Many writers are confused about the constituent parts of a paragraph; where a paragraph begins and ends; where to break a paragraph and begin a new one. For a lot of us, it's been more than a few years since high school English class, and a lot of what we learned in school refers mainly to nonfiction writing, not fiction.

In fiction writing, most paragraphs will reflect the structure of the story itself. In other words, fiction paragraphs consist of at least three sentences that have a beginning, middle and an end: the beginning sentence that introduces what is to come, then the middle sentence or sentences that develop the action, and the concluding sentence that does double duty by wrapping up the paragraph "subject" and also leading into the next paragraph. This is similar to what we learned in school about writing nonfiction: Introduce your topic in the first sentence, discuss or support the topic in succeeding sentences and conclude the topic with the last sentence.

But fiction paragraphs go much further than this. They control pacing by their shortness or length, draw readers deeply into a setting or character through more extended narrative, impart or withhold information, look back into the past or forward to the future, and utilize literary devices such as foreshadowing, flashbacks, irony, rhetoric, symbolism and subtext. In dialogue, each character's spoken words become a new paragraph, even though the conversation itself might revolve around a single topic.

Modern audiences, those who have been brought up on half-hour to one-hour television shows, two to three minute music videos and video games that reset levels every few minutes, expect their reading material to have that same quick feel, even though they are immersed in a 200 to 300-page (or longer) book. Shorter paragraphs help give a faster feel by quickening the pace of the read and opening up white space on the pages. Shorter paragraphs in the opening pages also help draw readers more deeply into the story.

In fiction and creative nonfiction, there are even times when one sentence can stand as a full paragraph. Like any literary device, though, single sentence paragraphs should be used sparingly and for special emphasis only, or they will lose their impact. The rule of thumb for fiction paragraphs: **at least three** sentences, more if needed, that have a story structure (beginning, middle and end) and that lead readers into the next paragraph until there is a natural break in the narrative, such as a line break denoting a change in time, place or point of view, or the chapter ends.

Besides hooking readers, first paragraphs must also set the tone for the rest of the story, showcase your writing style (lyrical and flowing, terse and abbreviated, humorous, ironic, etc.) and let readers know whose story it is and when and where it is taking place. Yes, you need to set up questions readers will want answers to, but you can't leave them so much in the dark that they can't get situated enough to relax and enjoy the story.

Remember those 5 W's we learned about in school? Who. What. Where. When. Why. This is what needs to be incorporated into the first few paragraphs of your story. If you can get the majority into the first paragraph, even if only as a hint, all the better.

Therefore, with few exceptions, this is how to set up your first paragraph: *Who*—your protagonist should appear in the first paragraph; better yet, in the first sentence. Readers will become emotionally invested in the characters they first meet, so let them meet the hero right up front. Don't confuse or frustrate your audience by investing them in someone who isn't the main character.

Then let readers know *What* is going on, what the character is doing —the action. Paint a vivid picture so readers can easily visualize what is going on. In conjunction with that, add *Where* it is happening: the overall setting—city, country, house, office, outside, inside, rooftop, alien world— and the timeframe of *When* it is taking place—present, past, future, season, time of day—so readers can orient themselves in both time and space. A lot of this can be detailed in succeeding paragraphs, but a hint of it should be contained in the very first one to ground readers in your fictional world.

Most of all, give readers *Why,* as in **a reason to care** about the character and what is happening. Make the protagonist likable, resourceful, smart and sympathetic. Let readers know what is at stake for that character by posing an intriguing story question that will make readers want to read on to discover the answer.

This is a lot to put into one little paragraph, but remember, you don't need to pack all this information in detail into the first paragraph. Your full "hook" is actually the complete Rule of Firsts: First Sentence; First Paragraph; First Page; First Scene/Chapter. Put only the most essential pieces into the opening paragraph. Each succeeding paragraph will contain a bit more of these essential ingredients, in more detail, as the amount of space available to you expands. The first paragraph merely needs to contain enough information to snare readers and pull them on to the succeeding paragraphs.

As for backstory? Forget about it until you have finished with all your "Firsts" (sentence, paragraph, page, chapter). **Backstory has no place in your hook**. In fact, it will pretty much guarantee you won't hook anything because it will slow down the action and give information that readers won't care about. Don't make the mistake of putting the backstory in as a Prologue; that gives readers a mistaken idea about the scope and genre of your story, plus it slows down the action and assumes readers already know and care enough about characters they haven't yet met to want to know about past events. Trust me—they don't. **Never** lade backstory into your openings.

Steven James, in detailing how to write an effective first sentence, paragraph and page (note he stops at the first page; that's the first 250-300 words of your story!), says an effective hook needs to do seven things:

1. Grab the readers' attention
2. Introduce a character readers care about

3. Set the story's mood

4. Establish your voice and style

5. Orient readers to the protagonist's world so they can picture it

6. Lock in the genre

7. End in a way that is both surprising and satisfying

If you can do all that in your first page, or at least in your first scene, you will well and truly hook your audience.

When we started this discussion, we talked about using the first paragraph to draw readers into **one aspect** of the story, something that is uniquely compelling about the story you need to tell. What are those aspects? **Unique characters** (think of Twain's Tom Sawyer and Huckleberry Finn); a **fascinating setting** (the Alaska of Sue Henry and Dana Stabenow); a unique writing style or voice (think Janet Evanovich); a **mystifying or intriguing situation** (such as that in Jeff Carlson's *Plague* series); a **deep emotional connection** with the characters (as with Elizabeth George's Thomas Linley). By concentrating on one aspect while including James' seven ingredients, you can avoid loading your opening with too much information that will only confuse and turn off readers.

Analyze the start of each of your stories. What is the **one most compelling thing** about your story—a character, the setting, the emotions, the problem, the action, your voice? Rewrite the first paragraph with that in mind and see what happens.

Exercise #5: First Paragraphs From Given Beginnings*

(Purpose of Exercise: To compose the first paragraph of a story opening)

CHOOSE ONE OF THE following first sentences and finish the first paragraph of the potential story. When working, consider character, setting, tension and story question (or the main problem the character has to deal with). Make each sentence lead into the next, and make each sentence so compelling the reader **must continue reading**.

Remember, you are writing **only the first paragraph** of the story, not the first page or scene. If you finish before the timer dings, choose another opening line and craft that first paragraph.

Set your timer for **15 MINUTES** and begin.

1. If only Shale hadn't walked down the street that morning.
2. It wasn't the end of the world, but it might as well have been.
3. I stared into her luminous eyes, entranced by the shadows dancing in their depths.
4. Gabby's foot slid off the ledge where she balanced a hundred twenty feet above the pavement.
5. They told me the morning I got married, and it shook the foundation beneath my feet.
6. Dahlgreddy came to fulfill a prophecy no one had ever heard.

Lesson #6: First Paragraphs From Your "Hooks"

THE LAST LESSON CONCENTRATED on writing first paragraphs from given openings. While not necessarily easy, it is easier to craft a first paragraph when you're given an opening that sparks just the glimmer of an idea in your mind. You can "dash off" a first page more easily because you haven't thought out the entire story yet, don't have fully developed characters with their whole backstory, or a fully-realized plot, or the sub-plots that further complicate the tale. It's a bit like being able to come up with really great opening lines when there's no story behind them to complicate their creation.

The same thing can happen when you come up with your own first-line "hook" and then continue writing the whole first paragraph—**before** coming up with the whole story. If it's a new, spur-of-the-moment (or timed-exercise-induced) leap into a **possible** story rather than one you've been working on or planning and plotting for a while, it's fairly simple—relatively speaking—to create a killer first paragraph. Again, in this instance there are no fully-formed characters, thoughtfully-created settings or painstakingly crafted plotlines and subplots to get in the way. There are only quick glimmers of possibilities, which give an endless array of directions in which to head, leaving the way open for some great opportunities to continue hooking readers.

There are two values to doing exercises like this one (and the previous one). The first is that you just might discover a really great story or two from these opening paragraphs. It can be astonishing to uncover what has been lurking in your subconscious, awaiting release, often tales you would never consider on a conscious level. Trusting your instincts and simply writing whatever springs forth—with, of course, the point of the exercise in mind—can open a fountain of wonderful story openings on which you can continue to work once the exercise is ended.

The second value is that when you learn through practice-writing how to trust your subconscious instincts when it comes to incorporating the necessary opening ingredients to snag readers, you can then bring that ability to the stories you are already working on, or have been planning to start. When you draft openings for new stories—or re-draft them for stories already started or planned—you begin to work from a position of confidence and strength. You bring to your desk (or desktop computer) new perspectives and alternative ways of expressing the essence of your stories.

This is definitely a case of practice making perfect, or as close to perfect as a first draft can be. That's why the exercises are here in these workbooks. I could have simply written yet another "how to" book, telling you what to do. But it would end up just another book you would read (maybe even all the way through), nod your head at, then hope you would remember some of it when you get around to your "real" writing.

But sitting down and putting into practice what you read **as you read it** helps to incorporate those principles into your writing repertoire. They become an intrinsic part of who you are as a writer. Then, when you finally start that story about Joe and Amy meeting in Paris ten years after their first disastrous date in Boise, Idaho, you don't have to sit trying to remember what you need to include in that first sentence. That first paragraph. That first page. You don't have to waste hours searching out the book that mentioned the Rule of Firsts—is it still on the bookshelf or packed away in a box in the garage?—or spend valuable writing time flipping pages to uncover that listing of seven opening essentials you remember skimming over a few months, or even years, ago.

No, by doing the exercises after each lesson—more than once, if you are so moved—you cement those techniques into your author persona. When you sit down to write your "real" stories, all the rules, ingredients and techniques will be at your fingertips because you have experienced them. You have explored them. You have lived them. You understand what they mean for you and how they can expand and develop the talent lying inside you. They become part and parcel of who you are as a writer.

So, trust yourself. You can do this, even if at first you stare at the blank page and panic just a bit because your mind is blank. If that happens, look around the room or out the window and focus on an object to boost inspiration. Or leaf through your family photo albums until something catches your eye. Then write whatever comes into your mind and let it flow from there. Don't critique, criticize, second-guess, cross out or try to do it "right." Just let the images flow as you incorporate an attention-grabbing first sentence, followed by the rest of the paragraph that introduces your main protagonist, sets mood and tone, establishes your voice and style, describes the setting, clarifies the genre and leads seamlessly into the second paragraph.

Exercise #6: First Paragraphs From Your "Hooks"

(Purpose of Exercise: To write the first paragraph from your own "hook" opening)

THIS IS A TWO PART exercise and will take about an hour to complete.

Part I: Write out at least eight to ten opening sentences that are intriguing and enticing, keeping in mind the eight strategies for creating great "hooks" (see Lesson #3). Set your timer for **12 MINUTES** and begin now.

Part II: When you have finished crafting your opening sentences, write out the first paragraph **of each** potential story. Remember that each paragraph should consist of at least three sentences and have a beginning, a middle and an end that leads the reader on to the next paragraph.

Give yourself **no more than** three or four minutes for each paragraph. This means that if you have a list of eight opening sentences, this part of the exercise should take no longer than **25 to 30 MINUTES**. If you have a list of ten sentences, you will need **30 to 40 MINUTES**.

Count up your opening lines, multiply by 4, set your timer for the correct time limit and begin writing.

Lesson #7: First Pages From First Paragraphs

THE ENTIRE FIRST PAGE of your story must be irresistible, not just the first sentence and the first paragraph. You cannot drop the intensity after just a few sentences. If you do, you will quickly lose the reader, who will put the story or book down and go on to someone else's work. Readers who are hooked by the first sentence and paragraph will almost always read to the end of at least the first page before making the decision to read on or close the book. Many will go on to the next page to see if you can "keep it up."

We're not talking the first chapter or even the first scene. We're talking **the first page**, which is somewhere between 250 and 350 words. That's what convincing most people to continue reading your work relies on—about 300 words.

Before you write and polish that first page, analyze for yourself what it is that draws you in as a reader. Imagine you are in a bookstore and all you can see of the book is only **the title and the first page**. No cover illustration, no jacket blurb. What would make you buy this book over any of the others in the store? Remember, you can only buy one book. So, what would most sell you on this one? Consider characters, emotions, setting, mystery/tension, voice, genre. Along with the grabber of the first sentence, the first page must also contain a "wow" factor at or near the end of the page. So that's two "wow's" on the first page, one in the first sentence and one near or at the end.

If this bookstore image is too abstract for you, get up, go to your bookshelf and read only the first page of every novel on it. Divide them into two piles: books whose **first page only** makes you **want to read on**, and books whose first pages make you **want to close the cover** and look for something else.

Now analyze those books that felt exciting, that you wanted to continue to read. What made you feel that way? Was it a sense of excitement, of mystery, of curiosity? Or did a fascinating, unique character draw you in? Perhaps it was an intriguing setting, a place you just had to find out more about, or the author's quirky fun voice that you just couldn't get enough of.

Now look back through those books that had the opposite effect on you. Why? What was missing on these first pages that you found on those in the first group? That is what you need to put on the first page of every story you write. Then you will certainly capture the audience you're aiming for.

Also, look for the **necessary story elements** that must be included as part of the first page. Did the first sentence grab your attention or did it feel a bit anemic? Were you introduced to a character you care about, or was a real connection missing? Was the story's mood set clearly from the outset, or did it wobble around before settling down—if it ever did? Could you tell from the start the voice and style of the author, and was it consistent? Did the author paint a clear picture of the protagonist's world? Could you tell from the very beginning what genre this story was in? Was there a surprise somewhere at the end of that first page, something that prodded you to turn that page and keep reading?

Check, too, to make sure that **backstory has no place** anywhere on that first page, unless it's just a mere hint that drops an enticing clue to future events. Too many authors load the opening of their stories with backstory that readers don't care anything about—indeed, they don't know the characters enough yet to care about their pasts.

Here's an example that I wrote, the opening to a book I'm working on. It has a "hook" factor in both the first and last lines; gives a hint of who the characters are even though only one is identified by name; paints a picture of the setting; denotes the time frame; and establishes mood and voice—all in 251 words. It won first place for creative nonfiction/memoir at the Central Coast Writer's Conference in 2008:

> The summer of '72 arrived full of promise and life. The sun poured blessings down as one day slipped past another in joyful parade. As a group we rented a four-bedroom cottage and named it The Boondocks. It sat on a bluff overlooking Lake Erie, in the small town of Angola, just south of Buffalo, New York. We gathered on weekends to, in the parlance of the day, "catch some rays." We played Pinochle in the sun on beach blankets and Strip Poker in the living room at night. We swam, went water skiing, built huge bonfires, drank cases of beer and raided local cornfields just for the adventure. Singles on dates had first dibs on the bedrooms. The universe was ours for the taking, and we didn't hesitate to grab as much as we could.
>
> Ted came to The Boondocks for the first time that summer, and fit into the group as though he'd always been there. In the three years I'd been married he'd blossomed from a pesky little brother into a

handsome man with broad shoulders, a tanned body and dark hair that waved around penetrating eyes and arrowhead cheekbones. He collected girls like wet feet collect grains of sand.

We worked all week and played all weekend. Young, healthy, invulnerable and carefree, we were poised on the crest of life with nothing but smooth sailing ahead. We drank in the wonder of being alive that summer. We had no idea how close we stood to death.

The tone of this piece doesn't need a room full of characters identified by name on the first page. It is enough to paint a picture of the carefree naiveté of youth, the lazy promise of hot summer days and star-studded nights, with the underlying threat of danger or tragedy lurking on the horizon to snare readers and make them need to keep reading.

The following piece was written in class. The "hook" at the end is more subtle than the one in the above example, but it still works to draw readers on. This opening is 294 words:

They found eight bodies in the ashes, but only seven of them were human. CSU Technician Jeremy Dace sifted the debris with care, searching for clues. What had brought the alien being to Earth? he wondered. What had it—he? she? did it even have a gender?— what had it hoped to accomplish? And who had set the fire that had destroyed humanity's first chance at contact with another race of beings?

The possibility of contact, the miracle of the discovery, excited him, even though the being was dead. He delved beneath the still-warm ash and found a hard object. His fingers closed on it and he tugged, but it didn't move. *Something melted into the floor*, he thought. He picked up a brush to clear away the ash. A voice stayed his hand.

"Find anything?" Jeremy looked up to see the fire chief staring down at him. "We got the Feebs, the CIA and National Security circling each other for a first go at this thing. To say nothing of the press. We gotta find out where this alien creep came from, how it got here, what it was planning. Lives depend on it, Dace. Who knows how many more of them are here somewhere? Or on the way."

The chief rocked on his heels, hands stuck in his back pockets. Water dripped from charred beams overhead. Dace could hear heated voices arguing outside the burned warehouse. The powers that be. Powers that would see only danger in an alien's presence on Earth. It would never occur to them that maybe the being just wanted to say hello.

He looked at the deep ash beside his knee, at his half-buried fingers still clutched on the melted object.

"Nothing yet," he said.

You can see from this that there is a "wow" or grabber—a have to read on—in both the first and last lines, a sense of place, a good feel of who Jeremy Dace is and the curiosity and distrust of authority that motivates him, the mood and style of the author, a hint of the genre (science fiction, given that there is an alien in the picture), and no indication of any backstory on why Dace became a firefighter, why he distrusts authority figures or why he is so intensely curious about the suspected alien. All this combines to make readers need to turn the page to find out what will happen. (You can read the entire scene in the Examples section that follows.)

Be sure to put in all the necessary elements that will grab readers as you craft your first line, paragraph, page (and chapter). When you do, you will guarantee that readers will continue reading, and that they will be telling all their friends that they have to read your work, also.

Exercise #7: First Pages From First Paragraphs*

(Purpose of Exercise: To write a compelling first page of a story)

USE THE FIRST PARAGRAPHS that you wrote for the previous exercise for this exercise. Pick the opening paragraph that appeals most to you and continue writing the entire first page, about 250 to 300 words. Remember paragraph structure (beginning, middle and end), and that each paragraph should lead seamlessly into the next one.

Remember also the elements that need to be included in the opening of your story:

> grabbing readers' attention (which you've done with the first line/paragraph)
>
> introducing the main character and making him/her sympathetic;
>
> showing the main character's need or story goal;
>
> setting the story's mood;
>
> establishing your unique voice and style;
>
> describing the story world so readers can visualize it clearly;
>
> locking in the genre.
>
> no hint of backstory

Also, as you approach the end of this first page, work to add a second "wow" factor (you will already have one in the first sentence; the "ending wow" is to encourage readers to turn the page and continue reading).

Set your timer for **25 minutes** and begin writing to complete this exercise.

Lesson #8: Collecting Brilliant Beginnings

LISTENING TO THE PEOPLE around you can lead to some amazing ideas for first lines for stories. For example, in a coffee shop one day, I overheard one man say to another, "I thought I'd wait an hour or so before I kill her."

I kid you not. I actually heard someone say that. I was so stunned that I left my table (with my laptop and purse unattended!) and followed the two gentlemen as they walked toward the shop's front door, just to hear more. Turned out they were discussing a recalcitrant marine engine one had been working on (hence the pronoun "she"), so I was able to return to my table before I lost any of my possessions—or any of my dignity. But I came away with a great first line for a story, so it was worth the effort. You can be sure I opened my word processor and documented those words!

Brilliant beginnings are all around us, if we but learn to pay attention to them. Keep your ears open when you are walking down the street and passing other people, especially those talking on cell phones. Most people have no idea how loudly they are talking, so it's easy to overhear them as they (or you) pass by. I've garnered quite a few snippets from partial sentences that I overheard in passing, which started my creative juices flowing.

Another great place to find snippets that can work into Brilliant Beginnings for your stories is to listen to those at nearby tables when you're dining out. I always have a book with me when I'm alone but, on the table, hidden by that book, is a pen and small notebook in which I can jot down the snatches of conversations that I hear all around me.

Often disconnected sentences will occur to you at odd moments of the day or night: when you're driving, working, waking up, falling asleep, watching TV, at a party, at church, etc. That's your subconscious thrusting itself up into the light of your conscious mind, reminding you that it's still there, working away at finding just the exact right words to open your stories, even those you haven't thought of yet.

Keep a notebook and pen (or tablet or smart phone) with you at all times to jot these little gems down. Trust me—no matter how fabulous they are, you will *not* remember them when you get home, the movie is over, you wake fully, you arrive at your destination, the service is over, whatever. (The hardest part is capturing those that occur in the shower, an environment not conducive to pen and paper or electronic gadgets.)

Sometimes these snippets will simply spark ideas that lead to perfect opening lines. Sometimes they will start off or finish a sentence that you provide the end or opening to. And sometimes, like the "wait an hour or so" one I overheard, they are perfect in themselves. We need to be aware of what happens around us, the words that float by our busy conscious mind, so we can capture those that spark that "OMG!" moment within us.

So keep your ears open for any and all little snippets of conversation you come across each day, wherever you find them, and be sure to write them down. You never know when one of them will spark just the idea you need to start you writing that award-winning novel or story. Or to help you find the perfect opening for the story you're in the middle of right now.

Exercise #8: Collecting Brilliant Beginnings

(Purpose of Exercise: To start a file of Brilliant Beginnings for stories)

SPEND TIME EACH DAY listening to the people around you—at home, at work, on the street, in restaurants, etc. Listen for any phrase or sentence that captures your attention and makes you want to know more, then write it down. It may be just a fragment, or it may be a full sentence. It doesn't matter, write it down.

Also pay attention to the stray thoughts that flit through your head each day, especially those as you are falling asleep and waking up. Those are the times your subconscious pokes through to touch your conscious mind. Keep a notebook and pen beside the bed to write these snippets or sentences down. Or use a voice-activated recorder, especially in the car so you don't have to keep pulling over to jot them down.

Make this **part of your daily ritual**, learning to listen and record what you hear. Start now, and don't ever stop.

Examples From My Class Writing

All these writings were done in class, with my students. They are presented as written, warts and all, with no editing. Please bear that in mind as you read them.

Lesson #1: Discovering Your Preferences

Best First Lines Answer Key (Author, Title and Date Published)
1. Thomas Pynchon; *Gravity's Rainbow*; 1973
2. Gabriel Garcia Marquez; *One Hundred Years of Solitude*; 1967
3. Leo Tolstoy; *Anna Karenina*; 1877
4. Geroge Orwell, *1984*; 1949
5. Ralph Ellison; *Invisible Man*; 1952
6. Nathaniel West; *Miss Lonelyhearts*; 1933
7. Franz Kafka; *The Trial*; 1925
8. Samuel Beckett; *Murphy*; 1938
9. Charles Dickens; *David Copperfield*; 1850
10. Paul Auster; *City of Glass*; 1985
11. William Faulkner; *The Sound and the Fury*; 1929
12. Toni Morrison; *Beloved*; 1987
13. Albert Camus; *The Stranger*; 1942

14. Ha Jin; *Waiting*; 1999

15. John Barth, *The End of the Road*; 1958

16. Virginia Woolf; *Mrs. Dalloway*; 1925

17. Kurt Vennegut; *Slaughterhouse-Five*; 1969

18. Toni Morrison; *Paradise*; 1998

19. Marcel Proust; *Swann's Way*; 1913

20. Felipe Alfau; *Chromos*; 1990

21. Brookner Vladimir; *The Debut*; 1981

22. Zora Neale Hurston; *Their Eyes Were Watching God*; 1937

23. CS Lewis; *The Voyage of the Dawn Treader*; 1952

24. Iain M. Banks; *The Crow Road*; 1992

25. Louise Erdrich; *Tracks*; 1988

26. Jeffrey Eugenides; *Middlesex*; 2002

27. Ray Bradbury; *Fahrenheit 451*; 1953

28. George Eliot; Middlemarch; 1872

29. W. Somerset Maugham; *The Razor's Edge*; 1944

30. Anne Tyler; *Back When We Were Grownups*; 2001

31. F. Scott fitzgerald; *The Great Gatsby*; 1925

32. Sylvia Plath; *The Bell Jar*; 1963

33. Stanley Elkin; *The Dick Gibson Show*; 1971

34. LP Hartley; *The Go-Between*; 1953

35. William Gladdis; *A Frolic of His Own*; 1994

36. JG Ballard; *Crash*; 1973

37. Dodie Smith; *I Capture the Castle*; 1948

38. Charles Johnson; *Middle Passage*; 1990

39. Sinclair Lewis; *Babbitt*; 1922

40. Raphael Sabatini; *Scaramouche*; 1921

41. Carson McCullers; *The Heart is a Lonely Hunter*; 1940

42. Margaret Atwood; *Cat's Eye*; 1966

43. Virginia Woolf; *Orlando*; 1966

44. David Lodge; *Changing Places*; 1966

45. Jean Rhys; *Wide Sargsso Sea*; 1966

46. Stephen Crane; *The Red Badge of Courage*; 1895

47. Jeff Carlson, *Plague Year*, 2007

48. Elizabeth George, *In the Presence of the Enemy*, 1996

49. J.D. Robb, *Fantasy in Death*, 2010

50. John Le Carre, *Absolute Friends*, 2003

51. Anne Rice, *The Witching Hour*, 1990

Lesson #2: Crafting the Perfect "Hook"

1. If only Cassie hadn't asked Andy to the prom, maybe she'd still be alive.

2. It started yesterday when Aramis chopped off the dragon's head.

3. The minute he saw smoke coming from the chimney, he decided to kill Malinda.

4. If it hadn't been for Paris, Jessica would still have her own TV show.

5. "Call me foolish, call me ridiculous, call me insane, but don't you dare question my qualifications, you self-centered jackass."

6. We should have locked grandpa in the attic long before the first snowfall.

7. If Joe had only hated me more, I could have loved him less.

8. Uncle Seth came to town the summer I turned twelve and I learned what life was all about.

9. Shouldn't it be easier to kill strangers than those you love?

10. Monica couldn't imagine why anyone would steal her handicapped child, but Leslie was gone as though she had never existed.

11. The sun came out twice that day before the world shifted on its axis.

12. The townsfolk thought it was a miracle, but those of us who knew better kept watch on the old Mason homestead.
13. If I hadn't loved him, his death might have devastated me.
14. Relationships with dead people aren't for the faint hearted.
15. "It was my fault that my brother died," he said, pointing the speargun at my chest, "and my fault that you will die."
16. "Ain't easy to kill," Garth once told me, "but you just remember, practice makes perfect."

Lesson #3: 8 Ways to Craft A "Hook"

1. **Something Unique:** Not everyone can walk on the ceiling, but I've been doing it most of my life.
2. **Something unanticipated:** The sky began to weep—huge, fat, cold globules that covered the land with blood.
3. **Deviation from the norm:** "Hey, Mom," I called, "isn't the sun supposed to be yellow?"
4. **About to change:** I knew something was wrong the minute I saw his face.
5. **Identify a character:** Annaliese sighed, threw the seventh load of the day in the washer, then prepared Evan's head for roasting.
6. **Middle of action:** The red laser dot held steady, centered on my heart.
7. **Emotion:** All I ever wanted was to be an aunt, but as I watched my brother's coffin being lowered into the cold earth, I knew it would never happen.
8. **Attitude or quirk:** Most people, you give them a couple of inches and they'll try to screw you every chance they get.

Lesson #4: 8 Openings For the Same Story

Story: Mermaid Eilish longs for the freedom of living in the castle that sits in the clouds above the ocean in which she lives, but in order to leave the sea she must find someone to take her place in the ocean. Then she falls in love with the young man she tries to lure into the sea.

1. **Something Unique:** The castle settled to earth only twice a year.
2. **Something Unanticipated:** He'd walked along the coast every day since he began working at the castle, but never before had he seen a woman peering at him from among the reeds lining the shore.
3. **Deviation from Norm:** Eilish's tail, much to her dismay, grew shorter the closer she swam to shore.
4. **About to Change:** Dawn arrived in a burst of golden sunlight, but the air hung heavy with ominous foreboding.
5. **Reveal Character:** Eilish, willful, impetuous and the fifth of seven merchildren, had suffered all her life from a fatal case of curiosity.
6. **Middle of Action:** She raised her head, stared into his amber eyes, and began whispering the enchantment.
7. **Emotion Packed:** How could this be her destiny, to decide between love and life?
8. **Show Attitude or Quirk:** *Tail or no tail*, Eilish thought, gazing at the lush green landscape, *I will not live my whole life confined to the sea.*

Lesson #5: First Paragraphs from Given Beginnings

Opening Sentence #3: I stared into her luminous eyes, entranced by the shadows dancing in their depths. I could see images: flames flickering around writhing bodies; buildings collapsing; fish leaping free of seething seas. Then she smiled and the images died. Her now-sparkling green eyes blinked at me, and I stood tongue-tied in front of her like a shy schoolboy before his teenage idol. What does one say to a person who carries destruction in her eyes? "Hello," just didn't seem adequate.

Opening Sentence #1: Shale shouldn't have walked down the street that morning—a lovely day, with blue sky overhead and warm sunshine pouring down blessings on the earth. Or so it seemed. Until Shale walked by, and I saw the darkness that followed her steps, the pall of evil that fell over the landscape as she progressed. Maybe it wasn't Shale's fault. Maybe the demons would have arisen by themselves. Maybe it was coincidence. But Shale walked, leading the destruction, and I knew I had to kill her.

Opening Sentence #5: They told me the morning I got married, and it shook the foundation beneath my feet. All I believed in, all I trusted, was gone. I looked down the aisle to where Case waited and cringed at the happiness and hope on his face. Would he still be there, still stand at my side once he knew? I had to decide: marry him or run away. And I had only seconds to choose.

Lesson #7: First Page/Scene

They found eight bodies in the ashes, but only seven of them were human. CSI Technician Jeremy Dace sifted the debris with care, searching for clues. What had brought the alien being to Earth? he wondered. What had it—he? she? did it even have a gender?—what had it hoped to accomplish? And who had set the fire that had destroyed humanity's first chance at contact with another race of beings?

The possibility of contact, the miracle of the discovery, excited him, even though the being was dead. He delved beneath the still-warm ash and found a hard object. His fingers closed on it and he tugged, but it didn't move. *Something melted into the floor*, he thought. He picked up a brush to clear away the ash. A voice stayed his hand.

"Find anything?" Jeremy looked up to see the fire chief staring down at him. "We got the Feebs, the CIA and National Security circling each other for first go at this thing. To say nothing of the press. We gotta find out where this alien creep came from, how it got here, what it was planning. Lives depend on it, Dace. Who knows how many more of them are here somewhere? Or on the way."

The chief rocked on his heels, hands stuck in his back pockets. Water dripped from charred beams overhead. Dace could hear heated voices arguing outside the burned warehouse. The powers that be. Powers that would see only danger in an alien's presence on Earth. It would never occur the them that maybe the being just wanted to say hello.

He looked at the ash beside his knee.

"Nothing yet," he said.

Dace let his curt words echo between them, then he pushed his helmet back from his face. "Course, we found the body over there," he pointed to the opposite side of the room, where another technician worked, "so I doubt there's anything in this area. Go ask Sullivan. I'll bet he's found something."

Dace watched the chief waddle his way over the charred remains of the room's furniture, then bent back to his work. He wasn't sure why he'd kept his find to himself. It could be nothing, just an ordinary household object destroyed by the heat. Why get the government flunkies all riled up over nothing?

That's what he told himself, anyway. Until he brushed away the thick layer of ash.

It lay gleaming against the sooty tile; round, about two inches thick, an effervescent purple color that seemed to sparkle in the emergency lighting they'd strung up. Too clean to have been through a fire, to have been buried in ash for hours. Too beautiful to turn over to the waiting authorities.

Dace poked at the object with his fingers. It didn't move. He used the brush handle, but it didn't help. The object stuck determinedly to the floor. He removed a glove, barely aware of his actions. Then he reached out and folded his fingers around the flattened sphere.

It felt cold, as though it had just emerged from beneath the polar icecap. It seared his skin, shot arrows of pain into his palm. He tried to pull away, but his fingers froze. He couldn't release the object.

Then it moved. It heaved itself up from the floor and into his palm, and clung there even though his fingers refused to fold, to hold it in place. It vibrated, a tiny, almost-nothing movement he had to think about to even feel. Thread-like tentacles snaked out from the sides and slid into his flesh. It stung at first. Then his hand went numb. And slowly, before his astonished eyes, the object sank into his palm until it vanished.

Dace's breath stopped for a long moment. He looked over at where various departments of federal testosterone vied for dominance. He glanced at the fire chief, still rocking on his heels, waiting for a way to screw the new kid in town. The lights all had iridescent auras around them. The people glowed with a faint green halo. Sound echoed in his head from far away.

A tremor shook Dace's body. He needed to find higher ground. He couldn't be found here, like this. He picked up his kit, pulled his helmet down, and made his way out of the building to his car. It took him a few minutes to remember how to work the controls. Then, with the chief shouting at him to stop, he drove off into the night.

Unit 12: Extraordinary Endings

"The opposite of the happy ending is not actually the sad ending—the sad ending is sometimes the happy ending. The opposite of the happy ending is actually the unsatisfying ending."

~Orson Scott Card

THE SECOND MOST IMPORTANT part of a story, after the all-important first sentence/paragraph/page/chapter with its "hook," is the ending. If a story is not wrapped up just right, in a way that is satisfactory to those who have read through the entire book or story, you can turn off your readers. They will not trust you to end another story properly, and will not bother to read any more of your work. And once you lose their trust, it's very difficult, if not impossible, to regain it.

Remember: In this digital age, **word of mouth is everything**. All it takes are a few bad reviews to tank a writer's reputation. What you want is to end your stories in a way that makes readers tell all their friends, "You have to read this story. It's so great." Never let them say, "Don't bother, the ending is awful."

So, how do you wrap up a story? It's not as easy as simply letting the guy get the girl. Or the detective solve the crime. Or the woman get the job she's striving for through the whole story. Or the man overcome the physical or emotional challenges he's been struggling with. Or the couple finally understand what love and commitment is–even though that is the main problem (the story goal) of the story itself.

If it were that easy, then there'd be no problem ending any story you can think of. And since solving the main problem (or answering the story question in a satisfactory way) is what the majority of writers do, most of the time they technically wrap up their stories in an okay fashion. It's usually in the nuances that the trouble arises.

Nuances? you ask. My ending has to have nuances? What does that mean?

It means choosing the right *type* of ending for each story. Yes, the guy gets the girl. Yes, the detective solves the crime. Yes, the couple comes to an understanding of their future. It's not *that* they do this, but *how* they do it that really counts.

Once you know you have a good ending, one that wraps up the story by answering the story question or having the protagonist finally reach the story goal (though not all stories have happy endings, per se, obviously you don't want a love story to end with the couple in divorce court, or a mystery to end with the puzzle still gnawing at the characters), there are **two steps** you need to follow. Ask yourself:

Step One: Does the **ending arise organically** from the actions of the characters? Are the **characters acting "in character"** as they implement the ending? Are **all the subplots or points wrapped up**? (There's one exception to this; see Ending #H below.) If you can answer 'yes' to all three of these questions, you have a good **technical wrap-up**. If you answered 'no' to any one (or more), you need to rethink how the story ends, then rework the ending so you can answer **'yes' to all three** of these questions.

Step Two: Once you have a 'yes' to the above questions, you need to then ask yourself which of the **eight methods** of ending a story works best for *this particular story*. Don't fall into the trap of thinking that one type of ending will work for all stories. We all have certain mindsets when it comes to our writing, techniques we gravitate toward, avenues we are most comfortable with. After all, we might be writers but we are still human and, as such, we are creatures of habit. But sometimes we need to step outside our comfort zone to find the exact right ending type for a particular story, a satisfactory ending that is **fulfilling for the reader**.

There are **eight types of endings** you can use to end a story with a powerful, even if subtle, punch. All are equally valuable in giving readers fulfillment and satisfaction, and in deepening the layers of the story you've just told. Being aware of the eight types of story endings and using the correct one for each story you tell can raise your story from merely good to "I won't forget this story for a long time."

8 Types of Story Endings (with examples from my own stories):

A. **The Symbolism Ending**—using a symbol to underscore the deeper meaning of the story. This symbol *must* be used throughout the story. (Ex: Iron nails are used as a symbol throughout the story. Ending: "She could still taste cold iron on her tongue.")

B. **The Observation Ending**—stating a conclusion that arises from the story's events. (Ex: At the beginning, a woman who was so average she bored even herself. At the end: "She certainly wasn't ordinary anymore.")

C. **The Question and Answer Ending**—posing a question about the point of the story and answering it through one of the characters. (Ex: In ending paragraph, "How had she survived this long...? Why had she wanted to?" is followed by: "She let her tears flow, let the end come. Ben's forgiveness was not enough, because she was at fault. And there was no pardon for that.")

D. **The Growth or Change Ending**—showing the contrast in a character between the beginning and the end of the story. (Ex: Story opens with a naive, happy ten-year-old girl named Abby. It ends with: "Wishing she could go back to who she had been, Abigail stood, went in and sculpted her terror in clay."

E. **The Philosophical Ending**—stating the point of the story in philosophical terms. (Ex: "If you don't give control to someone else, you can create your own reality.")

F. **The Twist Ending**—adding an unexpected twist at the end—though it can't be something that "sideswipes" the reader. There **must** be clues dropped through the story. This is almost always done in mystery/suspense genres. (Ex: A woman rigs an unwired antique phone to ring and drive a man insane, and then after he's gone and she strips away the rigging, the phone starts to ring.)

G. **The Closed Door Ending**—Basically an ending that says, "The End." There is nothing more that can come along after it. It's finished. (Ex: "There were times, yes, when J'npaire wished he'd been born a woman. This wasn't one of them.")

H. **The Cliff Hanger Ending**—leaving a portion of the story open for sequels. The major problem of the story **must** be resolved first. Only **minor** problems or aspects (a subplot) should be used to continue the story. Often, the characters' personal lives and relationships are used to continue the story. (Ex: After the main problem has been solved and the kingdom secured, the main female character is kidnapped: "Follow, my son," Priescence said as Jarrod strapped on his sword and stepped after the bird. "Find Oraya and bring her home again."

These are the eight ending types we will be working with in the following exercises. When you have finished, you will be able to wrap up any story in the very best possible way, so that readers will sigh with satisfaction and contentment when they reach the final words: The End. And then look for another of your stories.

Unit 12, Extraordinary Endings: Contents

Lesson #1: The Symbolism Ending

THE SYMBOLISM ENDING RELIES on a symbol being used throughout the story to illustrate a point, underscore a philosophy, stand for a character, etc. You cannot, obviously, throw in a symbol at the very end and expect that readers will understand its meaning. The symbol needs to be there **from the beginning,** appearing as needed throughout the story.

The meaning of a symbol is different from what it means in a literal sense. On the surface, a broken mirror is merely a broken mirror that needs to be replaced; as a symbol it could be used to mean separation. This adds a second meaning to your work, one far deeper than the literal one that is self-evident. It's another layer that delves into the emotional and subconscious core of the story—its **theme.**

Symbolism also imparts a universality to the characters, events and themes of your story. It helps readers bond more strongly with the piece because they understand, through the symbolism, how it relates to them— even if they are not consciously aware of that connection. Symbolism also gives readers a look into the writer's mind, at how he or she views the world and links common actions and/or objects to broader meanings.

Often, an object is used to represent another object, character, event or theme in the story, giving it an entirely different meaning, one much richer and more significant. Some common examples of objects as symbols are:

A smile as a symbol of friendship

A dove as a symbol of peace

A red rose or red color to symbolize love or romance

Black symbolizing death or evil

The symbolism of particular objects can change according to the context in which they are used. A chain, for example, could stand for imprisonment in one story, or it could mean the union between two persons or things in a different story.

One of the most widely known uses of symbolism in literature is Shakespeare's famous monologue in his play, *As You Like It*: "All the world's a stage, and all the men and women merely players..." Shakespeare equates the world to a theatre stage, and the human beings who populate that world are merely actors taking on a variety of roles throughout their lives. It's an easily-grasped concept for most everyone.

But an object is not the only type of symbol available to writers. There are actually **five areas** where we can identify symbols we can use to deepen and enhance our stories:

1. **Small Details:** Consider the colors your characters wear, the movies or TV shows they watch, the pictures hanging on their walls, the books or magazines they read, the pets they cherish, etc.. Each of these can stand for a deeper aspect of your character's life, events and/or the changes that are taking place.

2. **Motifs:** A motif, in art, is a repeated design. This translates in a story to an element that is repeated throughout the narrative. This

can be done in an obvious way, or less conspicuously so that it infiltrates a reader's subconscious with a web of symbolic cohesion. For example, in one story I used lattice work, as found in fences, pierced light shades and crocheted blankets, as a symbol for the way we live immersed in memories of the past with glimpses of the future instead of simply living each day to the fullest, as though it were our last day.

3. **Metaphors:** Some of the best symbols in literature are visual metaphors for thematic elements. Fire to represent a hot-tempered character, running water to symbolize purification, and illness to stand for sin or corruption come easily to mind. Strong metaphoric language often emerges **naturally** while we write our stories. Most of the time we are not consciously aware of them as we write. But we can learn to use them. Re-read your work carefully to identify those recurring motifs, then figure out how to strengthen them to better represent your theme.

4. **Universal Symbols:** Some symbols are deeply ingrained in our social psyche and we use them without even thinking about it. The danger, of course, is that because they are so common and noticeable, they can be seem like cliches. But with judicious care, we can use them to great effect. The fact that they have already been accepted deep into readers' minds gives them enormous power. For example, weather is an often-used symbol, such as a thunderstorm as the background for a character's defect, or as a contrast to a seeming victory.

5. **Hidden Symbolism:** Some types of symbolism will be so deeply buried that the majority of your readers may not recognize them at all. On the surface they have less power than the more obvious

symbols, but they can help enhance the atmosphere of your piece, and to those who do recognize them, the symbolism will be that much stronger. A good example is the name of Rochester's horse in *Jane Eyre*: Mesrour. The very look and sound of the name enhances the already dark and mysterious tone of the novel. And the origin of the name, for those who recognize it—the name of the executioner in *Arabian Nights*—only makes the symbolism stronger.

Finding the right symbols to use in our stories can be a delicate dance. We need to find the right symbols, those that will best enhance our themes. And we need to make sure we incorporate them into the story so they feel organic, not added on or overused, or they will lose all their symbolic value. If our symbols feel intrusive, cliched or forced, our writing will seem amateurish and/or pedantic.

I think the key is to **let your subconscious rule**. Don't stress over whether or not you have symbols in your story while you are writing. Don't try to plan them unless you can identify obvious ones when plotting out the story. Simply write your story, let your subconscious have full play, then go back and mine the story for possible symbols and their meanings in the overall scope of the tale. (That is what I did for the story that uses iron nails as its main symbol: wrote the story, then went back and identified the nails as the main symbol.) Re-write to strengthen those symbols, bringing one—the most thematic one, the one that appears **in the opening** of your story—into the ending to give readers a feeling of "full circle."

Exercise #1: The Symbolism Ending*

(Purpose of Exercise: To understand the use of symbolism as a story ending)

TAKE A STORY YOU'VE written or one you are in the process of writing, or one you have been thinking about starting, one that uses symbolism throughout the story. Or write an opening for a new story, or a new opening for an old story, that utilizes symbolism in the first paragraph (for example, the iron nails—in the form of nail-shaped shadows—that appear in the opening of my story, "Coffin of Silence").

Now, write a possible ending for the story (or if you've already finished the story, an alternate ending) that utilizes that symbolism to define the end of the story (ex. from "Coffin of Silence": the taste of cold iron that lingers on the character's tongue).

Set your timer for **30 MINUTES** and begin writing.

Lesson #2: The Observation Ending

SOME STORIES BEGIN WITH a very clear observation that is of a personal nature to one of the main characters. It can be about the character, something that he or she does, or the character's life, ambitions, philosophy, or beliefs. The opening might be something like, *I could never live without my music.* Or, *He always said the wrong thing at the right time.*

One of the best ways to end such a story is with the **Observation Ending**: by reflecting either a different observation at the end, or one that confirms the original observation. While it may seem too on-the-nose or obvious to us as writers—we are often told not to be too "on the nose"—for stories with this type of strong observation at the opening, an Observation Ending could be exactly what is needed to wrap it all up neatly for readers. This type of ending works equally well whether the observation at the end is the direct opposite of the observation noted at the beginning of the story, or whether it confirms it.

For instance, say you have a character who is an avid tennis player. You might begin a story about this person by stating, *Tennis was the most important thing in Carlo's life.* The story would then go on to delineate why the sport is so important to him, and show what else is happening in his life that will impact his dependence on the game. Maybe he contracts a disease that makes him unable to play tennis and he must come to terms with that. Or he becomes a "Big Brother" to a small, shy little boy and can only meet with the child during his tennis time. Or the new job he just got in order to support his family doesn't leave him any time to play tennis.

We'll pick one, say Carlo becoming a Big Brother to a needy little boy. The time needed to build a relationship with this child will severely impact the time he has to play his beloved tennis, because they can only meet during the times Carlo meets his tennis partners. So he has to give up playing tennis. Throughout the story he may struggle with resentment over losing his tennis time, and with regretting his decision to volunteer to help this boy. He may at one point decide it's not worth giving up tennis. Eventually, though, Carlo comes to understand what is truly important in life. The story might then end with, *And though Carlo still loved to play tennis, spending his tennis time with little Henry off the court far outweighed any pleasure Carlo got from the game.*

This kind of ending is dependent on **two things**: first, **a clear opening observation** on behalf of the main character that impacts that character deeply in some way; and second, the character's **growth and change** throughout the story that either makes the original observation no longer valid as stated and must therefore be restated to reflect the truth of who and where the character is at this new point in time. Or, if the closing observation confirms the opening one, it could feel almost like a cosmic joke on the character, or a twist of irony that gives readers a little frisson of pleasure.

An Observation Ending offers readers a sense of closure. It confirms that they "got it" and gives them the satisfaction of knowing that they understood the point of your story, brought home to them by the closing observation. It's the kind of ending that can bring tears to eyes, sighs to lips, or even a chuckle or two, and leave readers wanting even more of your work. Not a bad outcome for two well-crafted, illuminating observations.

Exercise #2: The Observation Ending*

(Purpose of Exercise: To craft an Observation Ending)

WRITE THE FRIST PARAGRAPH of a story that contains an observation of a personal nature to the main character. (Ex: I never get it right.) This can be a whole new possible story, or a rewrite of a story you've finished or are working on.

Then write a possible ending to the story that contains either a contrasting observation (Ex: I guess I did okay after all.) or a confirming observation (Ex: Like I said, I never do get things right.) that ends the story.

Set your timer for **20 MINUTES** and begin writing.

Lesson #3: The Question & Answer Ending

LIKE THE OBSERVATION ENDING, the Question & Answer Ending relies on a strong opening where a definite, clear and urgent question is raised in readers' minds. When you craft an enticing "hook" that pulls readers through to the end where they find the answer to the opening question, you have set a perfect stage for using the Question & Answer Ending.

The opening Question on which the ending Answer will depend can be in the first sentence, or it can be asked gradually as the first page unfolds. But it must be **clearly** asked, usually as an actual question thought not always, **within the first 200-250 words**. Readers **must** be able to know by the end of that first page just what, exactly, the story question of the piece is.

For example, you might open your story with a Question stated as one clear sentence: *Marilee, of all the pupils at Grant High, was the one not expected to graduate.* Readers will automatically re-word this strong, declarative statement into a question and begin wondering, "Will Marilee actually graduate, or will she live up to the expectations of those who thought she didn't have it in her and fail to wear that cap and gown?" The story might follow Marilee through that last, difficult year of high school, until we come to the ending that answers the question: Not only does Marilee graduate, but she does so with honors.

If you spread out the story question through the entire first page, you must make sure that you have instilled in readers the full question **by the end of the page**. You can see this done in the example in the *Examples From My Class Writing* section. Brisa stands in front of her church's congregation with arm raised to lead them in song, while inside she rails at what is happening to her, and doubts God's plan for her life. By the end of the first page, readers want to know what will happen to Brisa. How serious is the illness? Will she truly lose her faith in God and His love? These concerns are posed in the story as actual questions: *Why me?; Haven't I been through enough?*; and *What have I done to deserve this?*

When we reach the end, where the questions are answered, we find Brisa again standing with arm raised to lead the congregation in song. Through the events of the story she has learned what God's love truly is, and what faith and trust mean. And in what she has learned readers find the Answer to the original Question posed at the opening of the story, detailed in the final paragraph: *And she sang, "Amazing Grace, how sweet the sound." That said it all for her.*

All stories, of course, must have a Question at the opening, a story question that must be answered by the end of the narrative. And while all endings will answer that Question in their own way, the Question &

Answer Ending will answer it very directly. No symbolism, no subtleties, just a clear statement of the Answer to a very compelling Question.

Exercise #3: The Question & Answer Ending*
(Purpose of Exercise: To craft a Q&A Ending)

WRITE THE OPENING PARAGRAPH of a story that sets up a definite story question in the reader's mind. (Ex: *Marilee, of all the pupils at Grant High, was the one not expected to graduate.*) While all "hooks" should set up questions in the reader's mind, some are more obvious than others. Categorical statements like that of the example set up a concrete question and expectation for the reader: Will Marilee graduate? The story question can also be crafted as an actual question.

Now write a possible ending for this story with a clear answer to the opening question. (Ex: *Principal Snyder stepped back, read the inscription on the plaque and smiled. Marilee James, valedictorian of the class of 2012, received the highest number of scholarships to ivy league colleges than anyone in the history of the school.*)

Set your timer for **20 MINUTES** and begin to write.

Lesson #4: The Growth or Change Ending

THE GROWTH OR CHANGE ending is similar to the Symbolism ending, but it evokes more than just the symbolism. It also shows the change or growth the character undergoes. It can stand on its own, or be used in conjunction with a symbol that represents the character or the character's struggle. If a symbol is used, the symbol will **also** undergo a change that reflects the change/growth in the character. Keep in mind that **not all growth or change is positive**. It depends on where the story takes the characters.

This is a great ending to use for stories that are character driven as opposed to those that are plot or theme driven. When the story focuses on the character and how that character changes throughout the events of the narrative, the stage is set for an ending that underscores and illuminates the differences now apparent in the character.

The opening of a story that uses the Growth or Change Ending must detail that aspect of the character that will be changed by the end. The character could be shy and retiring, lack confidence, or be a bully. He or she may be arrogant, impetuous, given to gossip, a liar or honest to a hurtful fault—whatever flaw you design for that character. The opening **must** reveal in all its ugly glory the problem the main character experiences because of this character flaw.

The trick here is to also make this flawed character compelling in some way to readers, or the they won't care about the character. You run the risk of turning your readers off. It's not always easy to make a craven coward, or an exceptionally shy person, or a big bully sympathetic to readers, but you must be able to do so. You have to concentrate on the flaw and—at the same time—bring some hint of humanity and worth to the character that will make readers want to know what will happen to the character. It's a delicate balancing act: you can't make the character too flawed or readers won't care, and you can't make the character too enticing or the flaw won't work.

Once you have the reader "hooked" on the character and the flaw detailed in the opening two or three paragraphs, you continue with the events of the story, the circumstances that will force the character to face his or her own limitations or shortcomings and compel a change for the better—or the worse. The ending will then show the character acting differently, more positively or negatively, because of the growth and self-learning (or self-delusion) the character has undergone.

As I said earlier, this can be done on its own, or a symbol can also be used to underscore the change as it gradually occurs throughout the narrative. Symbols can be **direct reflections** of both the flaw and the change, or they can be **reverse reflections**.

For example, say you have a character who is a control freak, who has to have a finger in every pie, be the master of every situation, and make every decision for everyone. This character is being pulled in so many directions, is so constantly busy, that he can never slow down enough to enjoy either life or the people around him. If you want to also include a symbol, birdsong, for example, might be used to directly reflect this frenetic pacing, loud and raucous at the opening of the story, gradually lessening to one clear, lilting songbird call by the end, reflecting the way the character has learned to let go, relax and enjoy life and the people he loves. That is **direct reflection** symbolism.

You could also use birdsong as a reverse reflection by having one lone call at the beginning, a call that is barely heard and not even noticed by the character because he is so busy and self-absorbed. As the story progresses, the character learns, grows and changes enough to slow down and revel in the cacophony of morning birdsong as he sips his coffee on the terrace with his wife, instead of plunging into the day as usual. As he slows down, the birdsong escalates; a **reverse reflection** of the growth/change pattern.

However you choose to illustrate the growth and/or change in your main character—with or without symbolism—remember that at the beginning you need to concentrate on delineating the opening flaw while crafting a "hook" that pulls readers in and makes even the worst character somehow sympathetic to readers. And at the end, you need to clearly show how the character has grown in wisdom and/or self-knowledge and how that change has made him or her a better person—or a worse one, if your growth is toward the negative instead of the positive. When you do that, you'll have a story that readers won't be able to put down.

Exercise #4: The Growth or Change Ending*

(Purpose of Exercise: To explore the growth or change ending)

WRITE THE FIRST TWO to three paragraphs of a story that show who the main character is, and that details the character trait that will change (ex: the character is hesitant and unsure of self). You can incorporate a symbol (ex: a blooming rose) or not, as you choose.

Now write the last (or last few) paragraphs of the story, making sure to detail the growth or change that has occurred in the character, how that character is now different from the beginning of the story (ex: the character now has grown to be self-reliant and self-confident). If you have used a symbol, show how the symbol has also changed (ex: the opening fragrant, dew-covered rose now withered and neglected in a vase). Be sure to concentrate on how the character has changed or grown through the events of the story.

Give yourself **30 MINUTES** for this exercise.

Lesson #5: The Philosophical Ending

THE PHILOSOPHICAL ENDING IS an **addition** to the actual story ending, one that gives the reader space in which to contemplate the story and the message or theme contained therein. It consists of just **a sentence or two** that allows readers to stand back and let the full meaning tumble into their heads. The story doesn't end at the actual end, but ends with a **discussion** of the end, which extracts extra, or deeper, meaning from it.

This is much more profound than a simple recounting of how the character grew or changed that was the focus of the Growth/Change Ending. The Philosophical Ending takes the meaning of the story into the higher realm of philosophy and says to the reader, in effect, "This is what the story means. This is how it applies to you, to everyone, not just the character." The tense may even change from 'I' or 'He/She' to 'We' or 'You' in a philosophical ending, though it doesn't have to.

The Philosophical Ending is most often used in stories where there is either great antagonism for, or great admiration of, one character by another. The story will start out one way, say by the main character hating another character and, through the events of the story, the main character will come to an understanding of the other person to the point that this understanding fosters good thoughts and emotions, and perhaps even friendship. Or the reverse is true. The main character will greatly admire another character to the point almost of hero worship, only to discover through the story's events that the person is human, with feet of clay and faults just like everyone else.

At the very end, tacked onto the character's realization, will be a sentence—or two or three, but no more than that—that illuminates the wider lesson that applies to everyone—to the readers themselves—not just to the character in the story.

An example is a story I wrote about a woman who had been turned invisible by the neglect of her husband. His death freed her, and by the story's end she had regained enough of her sense of self to be able to manipulate reality on her own. The story could have ended with the line: *One by one they will all wink out of existence.*

It was a good ending from the character's point of view. But I wanted more. The story itself cried out for more. So I added a Philosophical Ending tag after it to deepen and underscore the main message of the story, changing the tense from "I" to "you": *It's easy; if you don't give control to someone else, you can create your own reality. Invisible or not.* The whole story felt much better, much more profound, for the two sentence addition. It acquired a deep, philosophical slant that had been missing before: Here is what this story means in the greater scheme of life. Here is how it applies to you, to the way you live.

Just be careful **not** to wax philosophical for more than a sentence or two. Long paragraphs or even pages of showing how the theme of the story impacts readers' lives feels to readers more like self-indulgence on the part of the author, and will turn them off. The Philosophical Ending must, of necessity, be short, sweet and to the point or it loses its power.

The Philosophical Ending isn't right for every story, but when you come across one that, even finished, seems to need something more, just a dollop of some inexpressible something, consider adding a bit of philosophy at the end and see what happens. It may be exactly what you need to take your story to a higher elevation.

Exercise #5: The Philosophical Ending*

(Purpose of Exercise: To learn to craft a philosophical ending)

WRITE THE FIRST PARAGRAPH of a story that details the actions or beliefs of someone the protagonist admires or hates. Then write the end of the story, showing how the protagonist now feels about this person, how the events of the story and that person's life/actions have impacted the protagonist's actions and his/her beliefs about self and life. Then add a one-to-three sentence Philosophical Ending that illustrates how the main point of the story impacts the wider world.

Set your timer for **25 MINUTES** and begin writing.

Lesson #6: The Twist Ending

THE TWIST ENDING IS the perfect way to end a mystery story, and when handled well can be an effective way to end other types of stories as well.

The twist is the moment of revelation within a story that **throws into question** all that has gone before. Most often it occurs at the end of the story, though it can take place anywhere throughout the narrative. In mystery stories, there is often more than one "twist" revelation in the narrative.

A twist focuses on one aspect of the story, be it a character's identity, perception, location, achievement, etc., then turns that aspect on its head. It reveals an **opposite** of the most dramatic, comedic, ironic or horrific kind. For example, wife becomes mother (*Oedipus Rex*), boy becomes girl (*Twelfth Night*), bikers become vampires (*From Dusk 'Til Dawn*). What you want in a twist is something that is **unexpected**, but that also is **perfectly logical** to the story.

There are **5 types** of Twists, four of which work for Twist Endings:

1. **The Identity Twist:** a person turns out to be someone or something else. For maximum shock value, have the character

who discovers the reversal discover it at the same time as your readers will. The longer an Identity Twist is put off, the greater the shock value to readers. But, as in all Twist Endings, there **must be clues** salted into the narrative all along the way, combined with a few "red herrings" to keep readers guessing.

2.   **The Motive Twist:** This is often found in crime stories, where deceit reigns supreme. We thought the character was after one thing, but he was really after another. The reveal **focuses on the motivation** rather than the identity of the character; it's a psychological deception rather than a physical deception. In James Patterson's *Kiss The Girls* (spoiler alert), we think the FBI agent is working to find the killer. In fact, we discover at the end he is the killer.

3.   **The Perception Twist:** This is the classic "scales falling from a character's eyes" as he or she beholds the world and all its schemes as they truly are. It's the point when the hero realizes the world is bigger/smaller/crazier/more mundane than he or she previously thought it was. Be careful not to descend into cliche (ex., it was just a dream); unless you can put a unique slant on it, overdone endings will simply turn off your readers, who are tired of the "same old thing." Also, the protagonist **must learn something** by his/her actions. The journey must be worth the ending, or readers will be unhappy with the outcome.

4.   **The Reversal of Fortune Twist:** Common to horror stories, this kind of twist is embodied within the events of the plot itself and occur through no fault or action of the character. It's often caused by an accident, an honest mistake or misunderstanding or simply bad or ironic luck. Because it has an element of *deus ex machina* (or

the author contriving events to make the story work, despite logic), you must **take special care to make the events believable**. If you can't imagine your readers making the same mistakes or having the same amount of bad luck as your character, it won't work for the story. Consider the advice by Pixar story artist Emma Coats: "Coincidences to get characters *into* trouble are great; coincidences to get them *out* of it are cheating." Because this type of twist cannot be used to extricate characters from their problems, it isn't a viable twist for a story ending.

5. **The Reversal of Fulfillment Twist:** What one character achieves another character takes away at the last minute. This is a result of both characters fulfilling their opposite objectives relatively unhindered. This twist only works if the main character achieves his/her objective first, then the second character achieves his/hers. A good example is O Henry's "Gift of the Magi," where the characters sell their most prized possessions to buy each other Christmas gifts. She sells her hair, he sells his pocket watch; he buys her a comb and she gives him a watch fob.

To be truly effective, twists must feel like they come out of nowhere, but are actually **foreshadowed all the way through** the story. Consider the movie *The Sixth Sense* (spoiler alert), where the Identity Twist at the end reveals that Bruce Willis' character has been dead all along. But instead of angering viewers, the careful treatment of foreshadowing by having something red in every scene with Willis, making sure no one ever touches him, and having one character actually say to him, "I see dead people," leaves viewers saying, "Of course, why didn't I see that?"

Make sure when using this ending, though, that you have planted clues throughout the story itself, so that **the twist is plausible, even if unforeseen**. This is **not** a *deus ex machina* technique, an ending that swoops in from out in left field. It is an ending that **grows organically** out of the story itself, even though the reader doesn't recognize it until the very end.

Exercise #6: The Twist Ending*

(Purpose of Exercise: To practice endings with a twist)

WRITE A SHORT SUMMARY of a possible story (a basic outline), showing the premise and the potential events that might take place. Now write the ending to the story, adding a twist at the end that takes the reader in another direction entirely from what they have been expecting to happen.

Remember when planning the possible events that could take place to integrate some subtle "clues" that will lead to the twist at the end.

Give yourself **25 MINUTES** to craft this story outline and ending, starting now.

Lesson #7: The Closed Door Ending

THIS ENDING IS THE equivalent of saying, "The End." It lets the reader know the story is done and has nowhere else to go. Should it not end at this point but go on, it would become a totally different story.

It's fairly easy to recognize a Closed Door ending. It often feels like an actual door has been slammed: Story over, the end, time to go home. It's hard for readers to think of what could come next, because it feels so done, so ended. Readers get a feeling a satisfaction and the desire to go on to the next story about different characters in a completely different setting, instead of wanting more of these characters in this situation.

A good example is a story I wrote about a character who both envied and hated women, called "The Collector." It takes place on another world, in an underground society. It starts out: *There were times when J'npaire wished he'd been born a woman. This was one of them.* It's an intriguing opening that draws readers in. They want to find out why J'npaire wished he'd been born a woman and not a man, and what was happening that brought that wish to the fore once again.

The story then goes on to detail his kidnapping and "collecting" of the "highest of the high," Council Regent's daughter, a crime that carried with it enormous risk. Once Drea's essence has been encased in a glowing light-ball and her body disposed of, J'npaire, exhausted, rests. The story ends with a slammed door: *There were times, yes, when J'npaire wished he'd been born a woman. This wasn't one of them.*

You can see from this that there isn't any more to come. The fight is over, J'npaire has won, and his manhood has been reestablished. If the story went on, it would alter the whole narrative's focus. The meaning would change, and the theme would veer onto another track. Perhaps J'npaire would no longer be the main character, or would no longer be the villain-hero of the piece.

To go further would change the story. Using a Closed Door ending ensures that does not happen. And readers go away satisfied with both the story and the ending, even if they want more. But the more they want is not more of this particular story. It may be more about the character or characters in different circumstances, or more of the world you have created, or simply more of your writing. As one judge said of "The Collector" (it took first place in the competition), "I hope that... you write a longer work with this world. Can a story do better than to make the reader both satisfied and want more at the same time?"

That is the main aim of the Closed Door ending, to satisfy the reader and yet make them want more at the same time. More of your world, more of your characters (though not in this exact story), more of your work. It's an ending that clearly states "The End" at the end, that makes readers sigh or smile with a sense of fulfillment, and that still imparts the desire for more. The best of both worlds, for a writer. And a reader.

*Exercise #7: The Closed Door Ending**

(Purpose of Exercise: To practice endings that say "The End")

Write a new opening or use the opening of a story you have written (and aren't satisfied with the ending) or one you are working on and haven't yet ended, and write an ending for it that has an air of finality about it. End it at the point where to go further would change the story so that it is not recognizable as the original story. If you continued the story from this ending, perhaps the theme would change. Perhaps the focus of the story would change to another character. Perhaps the message you want the reader to get would become something else. So the story has to end before that happens.

End the story just before the point where it would veer into another direction and change irrevocably. Work to slam that door, to have the very last line say, in essence: The End.

Set your timer for **25 MINUTES** and start writing.

Lesson #8: The Cliffhanger Ending

TOO OFTEN WHEN WRITERS first consider writing a story that spans two or three volumes, or even an ongoing series that concerns the same main characters, they think that the best way to get readers to continue on to the second and then third volumes is **not** to wrap up the main story, but to stretch it over the length of the trilogy. Or quadrilogy. Unfortunately, this is exactly **the wrong approach**.

Why? Because once you have hooked your readers on the main plot, they expect that the answer to the story question posed on the first page will be adequately answered **by the end of the book**. When it isn't, and they are forced to purchase another volume to see if it is answered in that book, most readers will have one of two reactions: disgust or anger because they feel cheated and manipulated. Neither reaction leads to them acquiring and reading any more of your writing.

This is because you broke the cardinal rule of story writing: **Never break trust with your readers.** When you make a promise to them, you have to deliver on that promise. And **the story question** that's posed in the beginning of every narrative **is a promise**. Readers expect, when they begin the book, that they will have their questions answered about the main plot: Will Susie win the starring role in the play? Will David and Marjorie get married? Will the detective discover the killer in time to save the young girl? Will the police arrest Miranda before she can exact revenge for her father's death? Will the aliens succeed in destroying the Mars settlement?

If the book ends when Susie is called in for a second reading along with other hopefuls, the church where David and Marjorie are to be married in the morning burns down, the detective is still a half mile away when the killer stabs the young girl, the man who killed Miranda's father is about to kill her, or the Martians are in the midst of the final battle for the settlement, there is no satisfaction for the reader. What there is, is a feeling of panic and disbelief: *I read all this and I **still** don't know what happens??*

If you have ever read a book where the story doesn't end when there are no more pages left to read, you know how frustrated and angry readers feel when this happens, because you've felt it, too. And I'll bet, no matter how well written the book was, that you didn't go right out and buy volume 2, hoping that the writer finally made good on his promise to finish the story. Were you willing to spend more money—and precious, unrecoverable time—**just in case** you wouldn't be so badly disappointed a second time? I doubt it.

Just imagine, then, how much more anger and disgust you would feel with the author if the story did not end with volume 2 **but went on** to volume 3. If you hadn't stopped reading this author at the non-end of volume 1, you definitely would after the non-end of volume 2. And you probably wouldn't be quiet about it. All your friends, acquaintances, Facebook buddies, blog and Twitter followers, LinkedIn associates,

Goodreads members, etc., would know exactly what you think of this manipulative author.

That's a lot of "bad press" for one unwise decision.

So, how do you get readers to devour a limited series story—or an ongoing series—if you bring the main plot to a satisfactory close in every volume? What do you need to do to make them **have** to go on, if you can't use the main plot to force them to read further?

The answer is simple. **Leave one of the subplots open**. (For 8 exercises on crafting subplots, see *Workbook #5: Tension/Conflict, Subplot*.)

The key here is to **choose the right subplot**, depending on what you envision for your series. If you want to write a limited series, say a trilogy (three volumes) or quadrilogy (four volumes), and then end the story completely, make sure you choose a subplot whose tension can be ramped up at the end of each volume until it becomes the main plot of the final volume.

If you want to write an ongoing series, as many mystery writers do —Janet Evanovich, Elizabeth George, Robert. B. Parker, Kathy Reichs, J.D. Robb, for example—choose a subplot that can run through the entire series as it changes and grows along the way. The easiest and best way to do this is to concentrate the ongoing subplot thread on the main character's personal life.

Always remember that **the main plot must be wrapped up at the end of each volume** of any series. It is only one of the subplots that will stretch throughout the series. This will give your readers a sense of contentment that the main story question has been answered—they did not waste their time reading only to not know what happened—and also a sense of urgency to read on to discover what will happen to that dangling thread. A win-win for any writer of a limited or ongoing series.

For example, your protagonist is a police detective who is at odds with two other detectives on the force. He suspects his wife is having an affair and his kids are out of control. The local bank is robbed and the bank manager is murdered. The main plot revolves around the police finding the killers (Story question: Will the detective find and arrest the killers before they strike again?), with subplots concerning the relationship of the detective with his co-workers and his family members. At the end, the killers are caught, the money recovered. The detective partially resolves his differences with the other detectives and discovers that his wife is not having an affair. But his 15-year-old daughter has disappeared. That is the cliffhanger that will prompt readers to get your next book.

This particular dangling thread could work for either a limited 3- or 4-volume series. The missing daughter subplot would gain in importance in relation to the main mystery plot until the final volume where finding the daughter would become the main plot, along with dealing with the aftermath of what happened, depending on whether she was found alive or dead. For an ongoing series, the detective's relationships at work could have great staying power as the series continues, and would be interesting enough to pull readers along. Or they could combine with the detective's private life, the search for the daughter and how that affects the family. Or perhaps the wife really is having an affair. Each outcome could lead to further subplots concerning the detective's private life as he continues to solve the main plot mysteries—the crimes—of each volume.

This is the direction that the above mentioned series authors take for their main characters. They weave the characters' private lives into and through the main plot of each novel—the solving of a mystery or crime—and "hook" readers on what will happen to the characters in the future. In many ways, the mysteries—or main plots—take a back seat to the ongoing saga of the lives of very fascinating, flawed and compelling characters. And their readers love the solved mystery/puzzle of each volume and eagerly await the next installment in the characters' soap opera lives.

It's also possible to leave a mini-cliffhanger at the end of a story, if you want to leave the door ajar to the possibility of a sequel, even if you have no real desire to write one at the time. I did this with my paranormal suspense novel, *Proof of Identity*. I don't have any real ideas for a sequel, but I love the characters and so I decided to give myself a little bit of room **just in case** I want to play with them again someday. The original ending was: *Surely whatever was in there could never get out*. To leave that door cracked, all I did was add two words: *Could it?* Now the door is open without setting readers up with a full expectation of a sequel to follow. They are happy that the mystery is solved and the boy gets the girl and happily-ever-after reigns. Unless I decide to play with them once again.

I am doing the same with the novel titled *Obsession* that I'm working on, leaving the door open to a sequel by adding a hint that all might not be quite as wrapped up as it appears on the surface. One of the characters is scamming the system, which could bounce back and whack the other characters—if I decide to write the sequel. But again, the girl will get the guy and hard-earned bliss will ensue. Unless…

It's also well worth knowing how to craft a good cliff-hanger ending because it's a great skill to have when crafting your **chapter endings**. If you can insert a cliff-hanger ending to each—or most—of your chapters, readers won't be able to put the book down until it's finished. They'll stay up all night if they have to, reading away.

Think of the times you said, "I'll just read one more chapter, then go to sleep," and then found yourself unable to stop because of the cliff-hanger at the end of the chapter. You just **had** to see what was going to happen, even if it was 3:12 a.m. and you had to be up by 7:00 a.m. to get to work. There simply was no easy stopping place for you to close the covers. You *had to know*. Those cliff-hanger endings just wouldn't let go.

I'm doing this in a fantasy novel I'm working on. I have 4 story lines that alternate chapters, and each ends on mini-cliffhangers throughout the book. For example, the Queen is attacked by giant rodents; the outlaw falls off a cliff; the Princess takes the wrong person's advice, etc.

The easiest way to pull readers from chapter to chapter is to end each one on a cliff-hanger. And the best way to ensure readers will read each book in your trilogy, quadrilogy, or ongoing series, is to craft a dynamite cliff-hanger ending for each volume that leaves an enticing subplot luring them on.

*Exercise #8: The Cliffhanger Ending**

(Purpose of Exercise: To practice endings that lead into a sequel)

THIS ENDING SHOULD BE used only if you want to write a series, whether limited on ongoing, or want to keep the door open for a sequel. It is never the way to end a completely stand-alone story.

Write the opening to a new story, or use the opening of a story you have already written. List the possible plot and subplots that might appear in the story. Then write the ending of the story, wrapping up the main plot but leaving one of the subplots open as a thread connecting to the next story in the series. If you're unsure of what to do, re-read the example given in lesson #8, above, or in the *Examples From My Class Writing* section on page 105.

Set your timer for **30 MINUTES** and start writing.

Examples From My Class Writing

THESE ARE EXAMPLES OF WRITINGS I do in my workshops along with my students as I teach each lesson. Please bear in mind that they are done in the 15-20 minute sessions and have not been edited or corrected.

Lesson #1: The Symbolism Ending

Symbol: a latticework.

Meaning: It represents the way we live immersed in memories of the past and glimpses of the future instead of simply living each day to the fullest, as though it were our last day.

Story: A couple, Christa and Jacob, have lost a child and are trying to come to terms not only with the loss, but also with their relationship as they try to hold onto the past. Throughout the story lattice work fences and lattice-like objects (the sides of the crib, the shade of a chandelier, an openwork crocheted blanket) appear whenever the characters become immersed in the past and their memories.

Ending: Christa spread the crocheted christening blanket over the photos that littered the floor. She could see snatches of the pictures through the lattice-like holes. Her life, and Jacob's, glimpsed now in pieces. A smile here, a frown there. A birth, an anniversary, a picnic beside cascading water. An empty place where Daniel once was. All relegated to separate niches, holes in the fabric of time. *Is that all life is*, she wondered, *a series of disconnected events that we try so hard to connect to ourselves?* Who had really lived the life on the other side of the veil? Not her, surely. Without these photos, she'd have so little memory of the events of her life. Even Daniel, his face, the touch of his tiny hand, the sweet smell of his down-soft hair, all of it was fading into the ether of time. *Perhaps it's time,* she thought. Time to break down the barrier, to leave the past behind. Time to truly live fully for the first time. She swept the photos into a pile, replace them in the trunk, then folded the blanket and set it on top of the pictures before she rose and went in to where Jacob sat waiting for her.

Exercise #2: The Observation Ending

Opening: *I couldn't live without my music,* Olivia thought. She took a sip of wine, then leaned back on the couch and let the gorgeous strains of the violin and cello wash over her. In a few measures, she knew, the brass would creep in from the side, echoed by timpani and underscored by the haunting strains of the piano. Schubert gave it all to her, as did Chopin and Beethoven. They renewed her spirit, calmed her worries and gave her the inspiration she brought to her paintings. Music sang truth to her. Without music she couldn't work, couldn't touch the truth, couldn't be an artist. And what good would living be then? The recording stuttered and she bolted upright, spilling her wine.

Ending: Olivia sat on the park bench, letting the silence enwrap her. Children nearby laughed their joy into the sunlight. She watched their mouths, could almost see the raucous sound emerge as great splats of red and yellow. A large white swan on the lake lifted its head and opened its beak. Olivia smiled at the glistening green ribbons that emerged from its silken throat. A young couple blocked her view, hands entwined, heads bowed together, lips moving in private conversation, leaving behind a scattering of pink and blue lace that dissipated on the sweet breeze.

Olivia bent to her sketchpad, intent on capturing the essence of what she was seeing, what she had learned over this last year. It amazed her when she stopped to think about it, but she was so much more alive now than when she could hear. She had thought that life was in the music, that without it all meaning would be lost. That she'd have no reason to go on.

But that wasn't true. She understood it now, and had more reason than ever to awaken people to the truth through her art. She'd been so wrong to believe she could not live without music. She could go on, and on and on until the end because, whether she could hear or not, she was never without music. It was the essence of everything, of life itself. It was everywhere, all around her. All she had to do was look, instead of hear.

Exercise #3: The Question and Answer Ending

Opening: Brisa stood in front of the congregation, mouth open to lead the singing, arm raised to gather the flock into the hymn. Which they started without her input, "Amazing Grace" being one of their favorites. But there was no grace for her, amazing or otherwise. Her high soprano didn't soar to the domed ceiling. She stood still, eyes fixed on the mass of faces turned to her. Sweat poured down her back. A white shimmer overlaid the scene. Her head spun and she knew she would pass out at any second. Just like the last time. *No,* she thought. *Not again, please, I can't take any more.*

Hadn't she been through enough? First her best friend's death, then her mother's, then the problems with her heart. All within six months of each other. And when she'd finally gotten her feet under her again, the pneumonia that had brought her to death's door, the blood clots in her lungs that made life a living hell, and then the cancer that mocked her at every turn, found because she kept fainting for no reason. Just a week ago, her doctors had pronounced her healthy once again. A premature assessment, obviously.

Why me, God? She cried in her heart as she backed up and sat in a choir chair, head bowed almost to her lap. *What have I done to deserve this?*

Ending: Brisa stood in front of the congregation, mouth open to lead the singing, arm raised to gather the flock into the hymn. Her high soprano soared to the domed ceiling. She smiled as she sang, understanding at last. It wasn't about being worthy, it was about trust. Trust in God. Trust that He was in charge, that He had a plan, no matter how invisible it was to His children. And He rewarded that trust, that faith, in ways a mere human could never imagine. She laid her hand on her abdomen, its slight roundness giving a mere hint of the miracle that grew within her. And she sang: *Amazing Grace, How Sweet The Sound.* That said it all for her.

Lesson #4: The Growth/Change Ending:

Opening: Emril sat on his stool in his dim workroom, hunched over the tallow vat. He picked up the rod and dipped the tied wicks into the viscous bubbling liquid. The scent of camben rose around him, sweet and haunting. It brought back memories of his mother. Which was probably why he hated to make camben-scented candles. Not that he hadn't loved his mother. He had, with all his heart. But memories of her brought back the horror of her abduction and his inability to help her, to save her. He was a coward, a sniveling worthless little runt who spent his days lurking in his cottage, making candles that brought light and fragrance into other people's lives. It had to be that way. If he ventured out, if he made waves of any kind, the Regent might notice him.

The thought made him shudder: The Regent, the man who had taken Emril's mother and then killed her. How he wished he could kill the Regent. Take a sword and run him through. Or craft an evil candle that would drain his life inch by tiny inch. But no. Emril was a coward. He had no value, no courage, no ambition. All he could do was exist from day to day like a quiet little mouse no one noticed, until his days were up.

Ending: Emril watched Meleia don the harness, settling the sword into the sheathe so it hung at her hip. Within easy reach. She turned her lovely iridescent eyes to him and gave him a grim smile.

"This is it," she said, her tone clipped, her body stiff. "Thank you for your help, Emril. You can go home, now. Back to your candles. Your real life."

Emril blinked at her. She thought the candle making was real life? She thought he could be contented to sit dipping wicks into wax for the rest of his days? He was made of sterner stuff than that. He might not always show it, but he knew now what he was worth. And it wasn't an easy life of candle making.

But he merely nodded to her.

"Take care, Meleia," he said, his words barely audible in the clear afternoon air.

"Good-bye, Emril."

Meleia tried to smile, but failed. He watched the pain and regret flash across her face, then determination filled her eyes. She nodded, once, then turned to the portal. Drinn slinked at her side as she stepped into the bole of the tree, wavered and vanished.

"Not quite yet, Meleia," Emril said. He strapped on his own sword, took one last glance around his world and walked toward the portal. He didn't know what waited in the land beyond the barrier, but he was ready, now, for whatever would come.

Lesson #5: The Philosophical Ending

Opening: I watched Adrienne stroll into the room like she owned all of creation. Miss Prissy. Her canny green eyes looked over the assembled throng with a covetous look I couldn't miss, and I just knew she was calculating which table would gain her the most exposure, the best contacts.

I think I've hated her since the first time I saw her, when she waltzed into Brad's wedding and stole the limelight from my brother and his bride. She always has an answer for everything, is always more clever than anyone else, always has the best ideas that let everyone know her cream rises to the top while the rest of ours hovers somewhere short of the mark. That she's tall, curvaceous and model-gorgeous, with a full head of natural honey blond hair and cheekbones sharp enough to slice cheese just makes it worse for someone like me. Someone who is simply average: average height, average looks, average intelligence. Someone who is invisible next to her.

Ms. Perfect. With her perfect clothes, perfect house and perfect life. I couldn't for the life of me figure out why she bothered with the rest of us. What could we possibly offer her?

Ending: Adrienne looked at me and raised her glass in a silent toast. I couldn't believe that we sat here, together, in true harmony. I would never in a million years have believed this could happen. And it had been my fault. I'd judged her from the outside, without even wondering what was on the inside. Indeed, I'd decided with one glance that there wasn't anything but a self-centered, empty-headed bimbo in there. Who would have thought she felt as insecure as I did? Who would have thought we'd have so much in common? Too bad it took us almost dying for me to figure that out.

I lifted my glass to her in return, and shared her smile. It felt so good to have someone I knew I could count on. A real friend, the first I'd ever really had. There's a lot of truth in that old chestnut about not judging a book by its cover. Or a gift by its size and wrapping paper. I won't make that mistake again. After all, a friend is a gift you give yourself, but you will never know how precious that gift is until you unwrap it and look inside.

Lesson #6: The Twist Ending

Potential Story: "Sonic Scrubbers":

On an alien planet being colonized by Terrans, a mining operation is in full swing on the other side of the mountain. It's a peaceful colony and the space cops assigned to the area are not the best or brightest. They get bored quickly and pay mere lip service to their duties.

Then one night they receive a distress call from their counterparts at the mine (who are the best and brightest), saying they are under attack by unknown forces. The transmission is cut off into static. The colony cops head to the mine where they discover everyone dead, their bones scrubbed clean and all organic material gone. All buildings have fallen, splayed outward. Strange lights stiff flicker in the sky.

Possible events:

1. The colony is also attacked while their protection is at the mine

2. Two children and one adult survive the attack and describe the beings they saw—humanoid creatures with tentacle arms and two heads

3. The colony cops, accompanied by the survivors, follow a trail of clues to a hidden space station in a nearby galaxy

4. In the space station they find detailed plans of attack on four other mining colonies

5. They try to alert the colonies but can't break through the static interference

6. They speed to each colony and find only one or two survivors at each of three sites

7.   They discover hidden messages being sent from their ship, piggy-backed onto their transmissions to headquarters, and realize that one of the survivors is betraying them with the aliens.

8.   They trace where the hidden transmissions have been entered into the system and arrest the first adult survivor.

9.   They race to the next colony only to find themselves in the midst of a scrubbing and barely escape

10.   They End up on the moon overlooking a planet called Terra, where the colonists came from.

Ending: I looked at the readout and frowned. Something was wrong, these weren't the right parameters. The bio-force rhythms were skewed, a rapid pulsating that cycled in a twenty-four-three beat. Not human. I looked at Corbin.

"Shea?" he said. "What's going on?"

"You tell me, partner." I dropped my hand to my disintegrator. "Why are your rhythms off?"

"What are you talking about?"

"You're not human, are you? You're one of them."

"You're crazy! I'm as human as you are!" He backed away, put shooting distance between us. "Come on, Shea, you know me. This is a set-up."

"How, Corbin? You tell me, how can the reader be wrong?"

"After everything we've seen, you need to ask? For God's sake, Shea, think! This is me, you know me, we trained together. It's a set-up. I'm not the bad guy here."

We stared at each other, then he went for his weapon. I was faster. His shot went wide as he flew into the air, half his torso bursting into molecules. Still, his shot hit my arm before it blasted apart the Reader. I stood there, gasping for breath, staring at the blood that ran down my side. The green blood. The children in the corner stood up. Krissa took a step forward as my mind cleared and memories re-loaded into my neural net.

"It's time, Shea," Krissa said, her second head appearing from where she'd banished it to the ether. "Time to remember who you are."

I looked down at the tentacles that had emerged from my ugly human body, and smiled. Then I triggered on the sonic scrubber and aimed it at Terra.

Exercise #7: The Closed Door Ending

Opening: Willa watched the other people who sat in the room with her. They all wanted this job, this well-paying job at a time when jobs were so hard to get. When there were so few jobs available, well-paying or not. She wondered if the others had the same responsibilities she had: three children under the age of six, one of whom was handicapped; a mother who lived with her, barely able to move after the stroke; a brother in prison who had to be visited and encouraged to take advantage of every program that could help straighten him out; two teenage nieces her no-good sister had dropped off six months ago and never returned for; a dead husband still sitting in an urn at the back of her closet because she couldn't afford to bury him.

She already knew she had little chance. She had only a fourth grade education, though she knew she was smart enough. She could learn anything if someone would teach her. Why would they even give her a chance when there were so many more qualified candidates to choose from? People who were better than she was. Maybe she needed this job more than she did. Who was she to try to take it from anyone else?

Ending: Willa knelt in the grass and placed the flowers she'd brought beside the headstone.

"We're doing well, Andres," she murmured, her tone as reverent as a prayer. Which, in a way, it was. "You don't have to worry about us any more."

She stood and looked at where Janine and Nelly herded the kids toward the duck pond that lay just beyond this section of the cemetery, Nelly holding Jason's hand so his unsteady gait didn't spill him onto the roadway's cinders. The new brace helped, just like the doctors had said it would. Even the kids at school didn't tease him as much anymore

Hope lit her heart, lifted her head to the heavens. They were all doing well. Mamma loved what she called her 'apartment' in the home Willa had found for her, in a place where she would be cared for with love and devotion. The girls were finally doing well in school, a product, the counselor said, of their feeling secure at last. There was food on the table each night, and heat in the winter. Charles would be released soon and take up his janitorial position at St. Joseph's rectory.

As for her? She wasn't the same person she had been just eight months before. She had found her place, both in life and at work. She had value. She knew, now, that she could handle whatever life threw at her. She had found reserves of strength she didn't know she had simply by doing what needed to be done the best way she knew how. A promotion. She smiled at the birds flying overhead. Who would ever have thought she could do the job, much less earn a promotion? And more money? In less than a year.

Laughing, she stepped out after her children, ready to share her newfound strength and joy with the world. After all, that was what life was all about.

Exercise #8: The Cliffhanger Ending

Story: Mackenzie Strait is a writer who comes into her psychic powers after a car accident. She begins to have blackouts wherein she "sees" what is happening between a kidnapper and his victims. She writes out the scenes, stringing them into a story for her critique group, not realizing that what she is seeing is real. She thinks it's an aberration of the way her creativity is showing itself.

Main Plot: Mackenzie gets closer to the killer, who also has psychic powers, and he comes after her.

Subplots:

1. Mackenizie's relationship with her best friend, Manda, who wants to protect Mackenzie from what is happening to her.

2. Mackenzie's relationship with Bass Ehrler, her ectoplasmic guide through the developing process of becoming psychic.

3. Mackenzie's relationship with the police detective, Carrick Dunwitty, who thinks she's full of shit and in league with the perp, but is attracted to her despite himself.

4. Mackenzie's relationships at work which are strained because of her emerging powers, which put her job in peril.

Ending: "I'm sorry, Mac. I should have believed you."

Dunwitty stood looking at her like a little boy caught with his hand in the cookie jar, but still sure of his own right to pilfer the goodies. Mackenzie snorted.

"You're not sorry," she said. She adjusted the position of her arm, trying not to let the pain show on her face. "And you don't believe me. You won't ever believe me, so why don't you just run along and do your narrow-minded law and order thing somewhere far away from me?"

Dunwitty's jaw clenched. He narrowed his eyes, drew in a deep breath, then turned and left the house.

"Mackenzie," Manda murmured, but Mackenzie cut her off with a glare.

"And don't call me Mac!" she yelled at the detective's retreating back.

They sat in silence a few moments, then Manda stirred.

"Don't say it, I know," Mackenzie said. She sighed. "I was a bitch to him. But he did almost get me killed, Manda. Him and his disbelief."

The light in the center of the living room wavered. Mackenzie caught her breath.

"Can you blame him?" Manda asked.

But Mackenzie didn't answer. She sat rigid, her eyes wide, her face drained of color.

"Kenz? What's wrong?"

Manda reached out, laid her hand on Mackenzie' arm. Her gasp let Mackenzie know that, as it had once before when Manda had touched her, the Arcane World had opened to her eyes. There he sat, relaxed in his maroon leather chair, slender legs crossed, ubiquitous wine goblet cradled in a long-fingered hand. Bass Ehrler. Or, rather, his see-through psychic projection. Translucent. Glowing. Smug.

"Go away, Fish Man," Mackenzie said.

"No can do, Mac." Ehrler gave her a saucy grin. "We have work to do."

"No," Mackenzie said on a long sigh.

"Yes." Ehrler took a sip of wine. "Are you ready for your next assignment?"

Afterword

"Always grab the reader by the throat in the first paragraph, sink your thumbs into his windpipe in the second, and hold him against the wall until the tag line."

~Paul O'Neil

BEING A WRITER IS a fascinating occupation. By its very nature it forces us to dig deeply into our inner core, face those things that frighten us, are painful or perhaps even disgust us. And then we bring those things into the light of day—on a piece of paper, whether physical or virtual—and transform them into a story that entertains, teaches and/or enlightens whoever reads it. It helps make the world a better place.

The amount of skill needed to do all that successfully is known fully only to those engaged in the practice itself. Readers come in two main groups: those who cannot conceive of what it takes to write a story, much less an entire book; and those who think it's easy to sit down and pound out a story or book in a few days or weeks. But only the truly brave actually attempt it.

Everything we learn to increase our writing skills helps improve us human beings. We learn how to see, to hear, to contemplate and to understand in ways that most others never do. We learn to find the weaknesses in our heroes and to use them to strengthen their characters. And, in a way, we are also strengthened. We search for the good in our villains and use that to make them human and comprehensible. And in facing our own dark side, we understand more about ourselves and those around us.

In this *Workbook #6*, you have learned 8 effective strategies for beginning your stories with compelling openings: first sentence, first paragraph, first page, first scene/chapter. Openings that will grab readers and not let them go. You've also explored 8 strategies for ending your stories, so that readers leave the worlds you create fully satisfied and happy they have spent time there with you. But you need more than how to properly open and end a story. These are only 2 of the 12 skills writers must master to make sure their work is the best it can be. The other 5 volumes in the **Write It Right** series will give you what you need to know, if you haven't yet acquired them.

Workbook #1 consists of the first three units of the *Write It Right* series: *Character, Setting* and *Story.* These are the first three essential elements of story telling, the foundation blocks, so to speak, for without compelling characters in unforgettable settings acting out amazing stories, there is nothing to write about.

Workbook #2: Point of View (POV) will take you through the murky waters of point of view. In its 15 lessons and exercises you will learn about straight, emotional and classic POV types, and the advantages and disadvantages of each one. You will then experience their variations and understand when to use which POV type to best advantage in your story telling.

Workbook #3: Plot, Dialogue continues your journey along the writer's path with 8 exercises on crafting flawless, intricate plots that sizzle off the page. You'll discover what plot actually is, the importance of a through line, how to analyze ideas for viable plots and where to find plots in the world around you. The Unit on dialogue presents 8 lessons that will show you how to write sparkling dialogue that sounds perfectly natural while still addressing the six necessary ingredients that make dialogue an integral part of the story. You will learn how to write for your audience, make your characters' voices unique, use idioms to infuse verisimilitude, how to tag properly and how to incorporate subtext into what your characters say.

Workbook #4: Scenes, Style/Voice contains lessons and exercises that will help you understand the 9 different types of scene structures and how each affects the rhythm and pacing of your stories. The Unit on Style/Voice will help you develop your own unique writing style, a clear, consistent voice that will stand out among all the others and be readily recognizable as yours alone.

Workbook #5: Conflict/Tension, Subplot will show you how to create and sustain the tension that keeps readers turning pages through 9 tension-filled exercises. The strategies contained in the unit on Subplot will help you add depth and dimension to your work by weaving fascinating subplots into your main stories. In this workbook, you will also learn the secret to creating an effective and compelling series that satisfies readers as it pulls them through one volume to the next.

And sometime in the near future, look for *Volume #7: Self Editing and Technicals*, an add-on volume to help with the mechanics of writing, editing and rewriting.

Look for the entire *Write It Right: Exercises to Unlock the Writer in Everyone* workbook series on Amazon.com in print format. Some of the individual units are also available in digital format in the Kindle store, but the workbooks themselves are available only in print because I feel that is the most useful format for serious writers. You can have the book open on your desk as you work on the exercises either by hand of on the computer, and not have to keep switching from one window to another to check on the exercise parameters or re-read the lesson as you work.

Thank you for purchasing this Workbook. I hope you find it helpful on your writing journey. If you do, please take the time to write a review on Amazon.com, since that's where most of my sales come from. In this digital age of social media, it's reader reviews that best help sell books. As does word of mouth, so be sure to tell all your writer friends about the *Write It Right* series, so they can also benefit from the program.

If you've purchased all 6 of the *Write It Right* workbooks, and have worked through all the exercises, it's time to start over again with Volume 1. These exercises are truly amazing, because they continue to work even as you continue to grow and develop as a writer. When you cycle back through the exercises, you find yourself delving down to a deeper level, pulling deeper meanings from your characters and situations. As your skills grow, so do your themes. Like peeling an onion, each round of exercises exposes even more of your talents and abilities, and takes you to places you haven't yet visited in your writing career.

Also, if you'd like, please drop by my website (www.SusanTuttleWrites.com) and leave a comment or two about the photos and story/character/setting ideas you'll find (Category: Woman of 1,000 Words), the weekly writing prompts that post every Wednesday (Category: Write Over The Hump), about the *Write It Right* program, or any other writing subject that comes to mind. Or email me at aim2write@yahoo.com. I'd love to hear from you.

Susan's Books

I NEVER THOUGHT, WHEN I started to write my own stories, that one day I would produce an entire series of workbooks on how to write fiction (and creative nonfiction, because these days that genre needs to be structured in the same manner as fiction). I never thought it even when I started teaching fiction writing. Getting my novels out was my main goal. But life has a way of guiding you down paths you don't even know are there, and this is where I've been led.

What follows is a listing of the books I have out in either print or ebook format, or both—and those in process of being readied for print/e-format. The *Write It Right Workbooks* head the list, but I'm also adding in my fiction titles at the end (suspense and paranormal suspense) in case you might like to take a peek at them, too (all available on Amazon.com and Amazon Kindle). I think they're pretty great, but then, as the author, I'll admit I'm a bit prejudiced.

My hope is that my *Write It Right Workbooks* will help unlock the talent and amazing stories that reside in each and every one of you. Happy writing!

Susan's Nonfiction Books

Write It Right Workbooks available from Amazon Print:

Workbook #1: Units 1, 2, 3: Character, Setting, Story

Workbook #2: Unit 4: POV,

Workbook #3: Units 5, 6: Plot, Dialogue

Workbook #4: Units 7, 8: Scenes, Style/Voice, Conflict

Workbook #5: Units 9, 10: Conflict/Tension, Subplot

Workbook #6: Units 11, 12: Beginnings, Endings

Write It Right Individual Units available from Amazon Kindle:

Volume 1: Character

Volume 2: Setting

Volume 3: Story

Volume 1-3: Character, Setting, Story

Susan's Fiction Books

Suspense
Tangled Webs
Sins of the Past
Piece By Piece

Paranormal Suspense
Proof of Identity

Anthologies
Somewhere In Crime (story: *"The Somewhen Murder"*)
The Best of SLO NightWriters (stories: *"Symmetry"* and *"Figment"*)

Coming Soon:
A Matter of Identity, historical suspense
Death in the Valley, collection of 3 award-winning short stories
Obsession, psychological suspense
Stealing Shyon, and adult fantasy
The Skylark Series: paranormal detectives
    The Somewhen Murder (novella)
    Dead Ringer (novella)
    Someone Else's Eyes (novel)
Destany's Daughter, volume #1 of The Unification, a paranormal YA/
    Adult fantasy series